THE TRAIL
OF FEAR

THE HEATHER REED MYSTERY SERIES

THE TRAIL OF FEAR

REBECCA PRICE JANNEY

WORD PUBLISHING
Dallas•London•Vancouver•Melbourne

THE TRAIL OF FEAR

Copyright © 1994 by Rebecca Price Janney.

Managing Editor: Laura Minchew
Project Editor: Beverly Phillips

Library of Congress Cataloging–in–Publication Data

Janney, Rebecca Price, 1957–
    The trail of fear / Rebecca Price Janney.
        p.   cm. — (The Heather Reed mystery series; #7)
"Word kids."
    Summary: Teenage detective Heather Reed investigates when
someone tries to force her friend's grandparents to sell their summer
camp.
    ISBN 0–8499–3631–4
    [1. Camps—Fiction. 2. Mystery and detective stories.]
I. Title. II. Series: Janney, Rebecca Price, 1957–   Heather Reed
mystery series; #7.
PZ7.J2433Tr 1994
[Fic]—dc20   94–33670
                                          CIP
                                          AC

Printed in the United States of America

94 95 96 97 98 99 LBM 9 8 7 6 5 4 3 2 1

Thanks to: Elaine McHugh for both her medical expertise and affection for Heather, Rose Hersey for her enthusiasm, and Dr. Scott—"yumtnoyboaim."

Contents

1

Unhappy Campers

N ow, tell me all about this mystery, Kelly!" Heather Reed exclaimed, her hazel eyes aglow. "You started to fill me in once before, but never finished."

Heather and her best friend, Jenn McLaughlin, were stuffed into Evan Templeton's Bronco, along with Kelly Fennimore and Pete Gubrio. The friends were following their church youth group's old van on the way to Camp Mohican for a four-day backpacking trip in the Pocono Mountains.

"I know that the group decided to hike at Camp Mohican because your grandparents own the place, Kelly," said Jenn. "But I also know that some kids' parents wouldn't let them come because of that." Jenn tried for the twentieth time to avoid a protruding spring in the back seat and failed. Both she and the offending object groaned in unison as the others laughed.

"Somehow, Jenn, I don't think you're going to take to sleeping on the ground," her friend Pete Gubrio teased.

"Or to hiking," she sighed. "I'm more used to lifting

French fries than my feet! This backpacking thing was not my idea."

Laughter filled the Bronco again. Heather had invited her best friend along on many of the Reed family's backpacking adventures, but Jenn always refused. Not even the prospect of spending time with Heather's brother, Brian, could persuade her otherwise. She was only going now because her choices for the weekend had been slim pickings: backpacking with her friends, or taking care of her little brothers while her parents visited Jenn's older sister at college.

The afternoon sun splashed over Heather as she waited impatiently for Kelly Fennimore to tell them about the strange events that had ruined Camp Mohican's business that summer.

Kelly, a junior at Kirby High, began her story. "My grandparents have owned the camp since 1950, and they've never had a year like this one."

"Haven't they had tough times before?" Jenn asked.

"Sure, but not like this," Kelly shook her head. "Right before Memorial Day the Pennsylvania Department of Transportation told them they were going to construct a new interstate that will connect the city of Erie to Philadelphia. It's going to hurt the camp."

"I remember reading about that," Evan said.

"How much land will your grandparents have to give the state?" asked Heather.

"You misunderstand," the girl corrected. "They won't lose any property. The problem will be with noise and lights, especially because the state's going to put an exit ramp right by the camp. That's what's most upsetting. Gramma and Grampa appealed to the transportation authorities to change their minds, but they wouldn't budge. My grandparents even started a lawsuit, but so many things went wrong all summer that they dropped it. I'm sure the state didn't mind," she said bitterly. "The lawsuit had them worried because it would hold up construction."

Heather made a mental note to put the state of Pennsylvania's transportation department on her list of suspects. *The planners of the highway had a lot to lose if the Fennimores won the case,* she thought.

Kelly nervously ran a hand through her short, black hair. "Then a seven-year-old boy was swinging on one of our swings, and it broke loose."

"I heard about that on the news!" Jenn interrupted.

"Me, too," Pete and Evan chimed in as Heather nodded soberly.

"The boy only suffered minor injuries," Kelly said, "but my grandparents sustained major damage. The parents threatened to sue Mohican, and every news team within a hundred miles harped on it for days. It was awful."

"I bet it sent some campers packing," Heather commented.

"In record numbers. Then, just as the publicity died down and the boy's parents decided not to sue after all, a bear attacked a teenager at Mohican."

"Oh, wow!" Heather exclaimed.

"After the attack I found the oddest thing," Kelly said.

"What was that?" Heather's curiosity was aroused.

"You know how the Appalachian Trail is marked by white squares of paint on trees?" The teenage detective nodded. "On one of those trees near the bear incident, someone had carved *C-H-O-M-I-N-I-S-K-A,*" Kelly announced.

"Chominiska," Heather pronounced. "Sounds like an Indian name, but I've never heard it before."

No one had. They couldn't figure out what the word meant.

"I asked my family about it, but they didn't know either," Kelly said.

I'd like to see that spot, Heather thought. "Maybe it's some kind of code," she said. "Kelly, it sounds to me like there's a conspiracy against your grandparents."

The others in the car agreed.

"All but our most devout campers canceled their summer reservations. There was only one kids' program all season," Kelly remarked.

"Were you there the whole time?" Pete asked.

"Uh-huh. I've been life-guarding at Mohican since I was thirteen."

"So your grandparents must have had a rough time financially," Heather pressed for more details.

Kelly nodded. "That's the truth. Mohican had always turned a profit for them, but this year it ate all their savings." She hung her head sadly. "It has eaten more than their savings, though. Gramma and Grampa used to be so cheerful, but now they just mope around blaming themselves for their mess while my parents try to protect them from further disaster. A week ago they had a family conference and decided to put the camp up for sale before it drives my grandparents into bankruptcy."

"I think that's awful," Jenn huffed. "The things that happened weren't their fault."

"I think the bad publicity did it," Kelly commented.

Heather steered the discussion in a different direction. "Kelly, you mentioned something to me the other day about a strange mountain boy. Then we got interrupted."

Kelly became animated. "There was this kid, I'd say about thirteen or fourteen, who'd just pop up at camp every now and then all summer. He was really weird, too. His hair was long and wild-looking, and he never said anything." Kelly shuddered. "What really gave me the creeps was how he always carried a bow and arrow. He scared the little kids."

"Who do you think he was?" Heather asked thoughtfully.

"Beats me. No one had ever seen him before. Woodie, who's our handyman and knows everyone, had no idea who the boy was. Sarah Cooper, the athletic director, didn't know either."

"This kid scares me, and I've never even seen him!" Jenn shivered.

"It's strange that he would show up this summer of all times," Heather reflected.

"Maybe he was part of the plot Heather mentioned," Evan guessed.

"I can tell this is going to be some weekend," Jenn sighed.

Twenty-one campers and five chaperons, including Kelly's parents and the parents of a girl named Katie Lynch, arrived at their destination just as the sun began to set. Camp Mohican's brightly colored trees waved a welcome as youth director Dick Walker introduced himself to the Fennimores. They seemed sad beneath their official smiles. Kelly's parents stood protectively by the older couple as if to ward off further blows.

After the youth group set up tents in a clearing beside the Appalachian Trail within Camp Mohican, Dick spelled out their weekend plans.

"Okay, guys, listen up!" he called out. "Since many of you have never backpacked before, we're going to take it easy."

Several cheers went up from the beginners.

"We'll have breakfast and devotions at seven o'clock tomorrow morning, and be on the trail by eight-thirty," he announced. Several youths groaned, and he ignored them. "We'll hike about seven or eight miles each day. That's an easy pace, and we'll never be more than ten miles from the main camp." He suddenly looked very excited. "I can't wait to show you the Pinnacle," he exclaimed. "It's a huge cliff over 1600 feet high. The experts think it offers the best view along the entire Appalachian Trail."

"What's below it?" Heather asked.

"A pretty, but wild, stream," Dick answered.

"Will we carry our tents and food?" Jenn asked, returning to more practical matters.

Dick shook his head. "Because that would make the hike tougher for the beginners, Woodie has agreed to bring food and collect our tents in the morning. He'll return in the afternoon with our equipment and our dinner. I had hoped Camp Mohican's athletic director would help Woodie, but other responsibilities are keeping her too busy. Since Woodie can't do it by himself, would anyone like to assist him?"

"Does that mean sleeping apart from the group?" Pete asked.

"It doesn't have to. The runner can help Woodie pack up in the morning, then hike with the rest of us while the handyman takes care of our things. At night the runner would meet Woodie at the trail's access road and help him carry supplies back to us."

"Could the runner stay behind at the lodge if she wanted to?" Jenn asked. Now that she had seen the great outdoors up close and personal, she had cold feet about sleeping in a tent.

Dick laughed. "Are you volunteering?"

"If I can stay at the lodge, yes."

"Are you sure you don't want to stay out here?" Pete was obviously disappointed with Jenn's choice.

"Quite sure," she answered.

"Jenn could stay with Sarah Cooper," Woodie suggested. "She and I both have rooms in the lodge, so she wouldn't be unsupervised."

"Do you think Sarah would mind?" Dick asked Woodie.

Kelly started to say something, but Woodie cut her off.

"I don't see why she would," he replied. "Say, I wonder if I could use that Bronco for these runs. The Fennimores had to sell their four-wheel-drive vehicle, and my car's too small to handle all your gear."

"Evan?" Dick asked.

"Sure," he said as he handed the keys to Woodie.

Heather liked the arrangement. *With Jenn back at the lodge, she can look for clues there,* she thought. *I'll tell her to watch everyone closely.*

After more questions and answers, the group toasted marshmallows, sang camp songs, and had a devotional talk. At ten o'clock everyone fanned out toward their tents, the guys an eighth of a mile away. Jenn accompanied Woodie back to the lodge.

Heather shared her two-person tent with Kelly. As they lay in their sleeping bags trying to get warm, the dark-haired girl said, "I have more to tell you about the summer, Heather."

"Go ahead," her friend answered.

But Kelly had grown strangely silent.

"What's up?" Heather prompted.

"I have the eeriest feeling. It's like someone is outside our tent watching us." Kelly pulled opened the tent flap gingerly. Then she gasped. "Heather, it's *him!*"

2

Scream in the Dark

"What is it?" Heather demanded.

"It was the mountain boy!" Kelly replied shakily.

"I'm going after him," Heather announced, climbing out of her sleeping bag.

"Please be careful!" Kelly pleaded. "He may be dangerous."

Heather bolted through the canvas tent flap and listened for the mountain boy's footsteps. *I can't tell which way he went,* she thought in frustration. It was very dark. Suddenly Heather saw a light flicker nearby. Just as she started making a run toward it, however, a hand grabbed her arm. Fear surged through her.

"Heather! What's going on?" a woman demanded.

It was Kelly's mother, Arlene Fennimore.

"Oh, Mrs. Fennimore, someone was outside our tent, and I'm trying to see who it was," she stammered.

"Mom?" Kelly poked her head through the tent's opening. "I saw that mountain boy again."

"There is no mountain boy!" the woman snapped.

She put her hands on her hips and glared at her daughter.

Mrs. Fennimore's emotional response intrigued Heather, who, by now, had given up on chasing the boy. "You don't think there is such a person, then?" she asked.

"No, I do not," Mrs. Fennimore responded firmly. "Some bizarre things happened over the summer, and Kelly's imagination ran wild."

"I just wish you'd believe me," her daughter said sadly.

"It doesn't matter anymore. Gramma and Grampa just told me they sold the camp."

"What! Oh, it can't be!" Kelly put her head in her hands.

"Now, girls, settle down. We have a big day ahead of us tomorrow," her mother said.

Heather crawled back into her sleeping bag.

"It's all over," Kelly wept softly. "Just forget I even asked you to help."

"I'm not giving up yet," her friend said. "If someone is sabotaging this camp, I'll find out."

"Sure," Kelly said sarcastically, "if Mom lets you."

In the silence that followed, Heather thought about the Fennimore family. *Kelly's grandparents seemed so negative tonight,* she mused. *They kept saying things like, "That's life. What can you do about it?" Then Kelly's parents just tried to smooth things over.* Heather rolled over. *I wonder who bought the camp. And who is this*

*mountain boy anyway? I'm more curious than ever
about this place!*

On Friday morning Heather awakened earlier than the
other campers. She went into the hemlocks, looking for
the mountain boy's footprints or any other clue he might
have left behind. She found nothing. Then she told Kelly
about her search.

"I saw him! You've got to believe me!" Kelly insisted.

"I do," Heather replied. "I'm just amazed that the boy
is that stealthy. He truly knows these mountains."

Kelly exhaled loudly. "I'm so glad you understand,
Heather. You're my last hope. My mother has been just
awful about this. At times I wonder if I am just imagin-
ing things."

"Why does your mom get so upset about this boy?"

"I guess it's because she's trying to protect Gramma
and Grampa from all that's been happening. She's really
worried about them. Her parents died when she was
young, and she treats Dad's folks as if they're her own."
Kelly grinned. "Sometimes I think Mom's trying to worry
FOR them."

"That's tough," Heather commented. Then she said,
"What were you going to tell me last night when you
saw that boy?"

"I can't now," she replied. "If we don't hurry up, we'll
be late for breakfast, and Dick will have our heads."

Over a hearty meal of sausage, eggs, and pancakes,

Heather and Kelly told Jenn about the mountain boy's appearance.

"I was up all night after that," Kelly remarked. "Of course, the rocks under my sleeping bag didn't help."

"Sounds awful!" Jenn shivered. "I'm just glad I'm staying at the lodge, even if Sarah hardly talks to me. I don't think she wants me there. I . . . "

Jenn was interrupted by Dick Walker's call to gather around. Then he showed the group where they would hike that day.

"Before lunch we'll do the four-mile part of the Appalachian Trail that cuts through Camp Mohican." He pointed to a map. "Then we'll cover another three miles this afternoon. It's quite easy. Okay, everyone, take down your tents, and help Woodie and Jenn pack up the Bronco! It's time to move out!"

"I guess I'll see you tonight," Jenn smiled. "Have fun!"

"You too," Heather said. "Remember, keep your eyes open."

"I will," her redheaded friend promised.

For those who had never taken to the trail before, the day brought a challenge. The youth group members who backpacked regularly tried not to walk too fast, but the rookies kept falling behind. Although Heather was one of the experts, she stayed with the beginners. The grumbling started before lunch and boiled over at dinner.

"I have sore feet," Sushmita Sindwani, a girl from India, complained quietly.

"So do I," her brother agreed.

"I just wish there was a bathroom," moaned Katie Lynch.

By suppertime the murmuring had magnified.

"Am I ever glad I volunteered to help Woodie!" Jenn exclaimed after polishing off two hamburgers. "Everyone's complaining!"

"I know," Pete said. "It's been a rough day."

"I thought I'd die of boredom if Dick pointed out one more tree the porcupines had stripped," Catherine Nitzel, a beginner, remarked.

"You didn't like that 'sound-off' song either," her boyfriend, Bill Barton, teased.

"It's been going through my head all day long," she groaned as the others laughed.

"I guess the beaver dam didn't excite you either?" Evan joked.

"I do admit that when the beaver finally came—after we waited and waited and waited—it was cute," she grinned.

"Do people backpack in India?" Kelly asked Sushmita.

"Not my people!" Everyone laughed. "I am enjoying myself, though," she said. "Except for my hurting feet."

As the group broke into various smaller parties around the campfire after dinner, Kelly finished telling Heather, Jenn, Pete, and Evan the rest of the mystery.

"Are you staying here tonight or going back to Sarah Cooper's apartment?" Pete asked Jenn.

"Going back," she said, licking marshmallow goo from her fingers. "But Woodie's talking up a storm over there with Mr. Lynch," she pointed out, "so I don't have to leave yet. Man, can Woodie tell war stories!"

"Like I started telling you earlier, weird things happened around camp this summer," Kelly began.

"Like what?" Evan prodded.

"Well, I already told you about the new interstate and the mountain boy." She glanced around to make sure her mother wasn't nearby. "I forgot to mention that Sarah Cooper's brother, Duncan, works for the Pennsylvania Department of Transportation. He came around a few times and had some heated arguments with his sister."

"About what?" Heather was intensely curious.

"I never could find out," she admitted. "What I do know is that he tried to talk my grandparents out of their lawsuit against the state."

"Sounds suspicious to me," Jenn mused.

"And to me, too," Heather agreed.

"There's more," Kelly went on. "A few times during the summer, the food Gramma and Grampa ordered for the camp didn't get delivered."

"Didn't your grandparents complain?" asked Pete.

"They sure did. But the company told them the orders had been canceled," Kelly said. "The manager said that if they canceled their orders again, he'd close their account."

"That's weird," Evan remarked. "Who do you think axed the orders?"

"We don't know. Neither of my grandparents canceled them, that's for sure." Kelly paused. "Then there was

Sarah." Jenn looked at her sideways, and Kelly met her gaze. "Keep an eye on her, Jenn," she warned.

"Why?" Jenn began to wonder whether she might not be safer on the trail after all.

"Sarah started working here two years ago as athletic director after she graduated from college. At first I liked her a lot. We even hung out together last summer." Kelly sighed. "This year she treated me like I had an incurable disease!"

"What happened?" Heather queried.

"I'm not sure, but Sarah got real moody, especially after her brother visited."

"Maybe he was plotting against your grandparents and wanted her to help him," Evan suggested.

Kelly also said that the press had hounded her family all summer, even after the swing and bear incidents. "Reporters kept tracking down rumors about the camp, rumors that apparently came from an unidentified source at the state level. One day I asked Sarah's brother about it. He denied knowing anything." Kelly's eyes flashed. "I think he was lying."

Heather made a mental note of that.

"There's more," Kelly continued. "Gramma and Grampa received harassing mail and phone calls."

"Were they ever traced?" Heather questioned.

"The mail usually came from nearby towns, but it was never signed and didn't include return addresses," Kelly said. "The callers were never identified either."

"What a summer you had!" Pete exclaimed.

"I'll say," Evan agreed.

"I'm not finished yet," Kelly warned. "The next thing that went wrong was when the Humane Society came after someone complained anonymously about our horses being mistreated. After that, a health inspector made a surprise visit to the kitchen and found it unsanitary."

"Was it really?" Evan asked.

"No way! My mom and dad were on duty that day. They had come during their vacation to relieve my grandparents. While my folks responded to a drowning scare at the lake, someone trashed the kitchen."

Pete whistled.

"And guess what else?" Kelly looked around at everyone as she paused. "Duncan Cooper was visiting that day."

"That seems suspicious," Heather commented.

"Please do your best to get to the bottom of this, Heather," Kelly pleaded. "Maybe it still isn't too late. The actual sale of Camp Mohican won't be settled for another five weeks."

"I'll do everything I can," Heather pledged.

"We will, too," the others promised.

After Woodie and Jenn unloaded and helped set up the tents, the handyman took her back to the lodge. The entire group fell asleep quickly following their full day of hiking, fresh air, and good food. But at midnight, a piercing scream awakened everyone!

3

Creatures Great and Small

What was that?" Kelly Fennimore cried out.

Heather was already out of her sleeping bag. "Let's find out!" she urged, groping for her shoes.

Kelly slipped out of her bedroll as the teenage detective unzipped the tent flap. Several heads poked out of surrounding tents, and the girls began talking all at once.

"What was that?" Katie Lynch hollered.

"What happened?" Mrs. Fennimore demanded as she left her tent.

"It sounded like a man screaming," Kelly said.

A moment later Heather added, "It sounded like more than one. We'll check things out, Mrs. Fennimore," she announced, eager to find out what was happening.

"You're not going over there without me," the dark-haired woman told her firmly.

"Please hurry," Heather coaxed as she and Kelly headed toward the guys' area fifty yards away in the next clearing.

Moments later Heather, Kelly, and Arlene Fennimore found the guys' camp in a state of chaos.

"There it is!" someone cried out.

"Grab it, will ya?" another guy demanded.

"Now it's on me!"

"Hold still!"

"Is it poisonous?"

"What in the world is going on?" Mrs. Fennimore asked her husband as he tried to restore order.

"There's a snake on the loose," Mr. Fennimore explained.

"A snake!" Kelly wailed, backing away. "Oh, I hate snakes!"

Heather drew closer and saw that Evan and Pete had cornered the reptile.

"Easy does it," Dick Walker advised. Heather noticed how pale he looked.

Pete finally managed to spear the snake with his pointed walking stick. "It's a copperhead," he revealed, holding it away from him. "I think we'd better kill it or it may hurt someone."

"I'll help," Evan offered. "I know what to do."

"Just be careful," Dick cautioned as everyone pointed at the snake and talked all at once.

"Are you all right?" Heather asked Dick.

"Yes, I'm all right!" he snapped. He was instantly sorry for his angry words. "Sorry about that, Heather. I'm feeling pretty uptight."

"What happened?" Mrs. Fennimore asked, and everyone started talking, telling their versions of the snake story.

"Hey, guys, let's calm down," Dick hollered. When he could be heard again, he explained how the whole mess had started. "I left my tent about ten minutes ago because I saw a light coming from those trees." Dick pointed to a stand of hemlocks just across the trail from their encampment. "I thought some of the guys were over there goofing off."

"But they weren't?" Heather prodded.

Mr. Lynch interrupted. "Nope. I made sure they were all in their tents before I got into mine. Then I stayed awake and read for a while. I was still up when I heard Dick yell."

"Did you see the light, Mr. Lynch?" Heather asked Katie's dad.

"I didn't see anything, but my tent faces the other direction," he explained.

"Well, I stood there for a minute looking around," Dick continued. "Then all of a sudden I heard footsteps, and this snake came flying at me. It hit me right in the chest. I thought someone was playing a practical joke on me."

"Gross!" Kelly said in disgust.

Instantly the male campers defended their innocence. Because of Mr. Lynch's statement that he had seen them all to their tents, Dick was inclined to believe the teenagers.

"Quiet!" Mrs. Fennimore clapped her hands several times. When she could be heard she asked, "From what direction did the snake come?"

"From over there." Dick pointed to the clearing just to the right of his tent.

"What happened to that light?" Heather inquired.

"It just went away."

"Before or after the snake hit you?" she persisted. Heather had the distinct impression that the whole situation had been a set-up designed to scare the youth group off the trail.

"Uh, before, I think."

"Well, it's all over now, so everyone can just go back to bed." Mrs. Fennimore started shooing the guys back to their tents, including Evan and Pete, who had just returned from destroying the venomous snake.

While she, her husband, and Mr. Lynch helped get the guys calmed down, Heather and Kelly continued discussing the situation with Dick.

"I think the whole thing was a nasty trick," the youth director said, "but who did it? None of our guys could have." After a brief pause he asked, "Kelly, could this have something to do with Camp Mohican's problems?"

She nodded solemnly. "I think so."

"Let's look for clues," Heather suggested. "We have a few minutes before your mom finishes up, Kelly."

"I'm game," she said eagerly.

"Me, too," Dick agreed. "I'll show you where I saw that light." He found his flashlight on the ground near his tent. It lay where he had dropped it after someone had thrown the snake at him. Heather and Kelly each had their own flashlights.

"Do you think someone was trying to get your attention?" Heather asked Dick, sniffing for evidence like a bloodhound.

"I did have that impression," he stated.

Heather was an expert at detecting the most minute clues, and her skills did not fail her this time. Within seconds she had found an inscription on a tree near Dick's tent. It was the word *chominiska!*

"There's that word again!" Kelly announced.

"Is this the place you told me about where they saw the bear strike last summer?" Heather asked.

Her friend looked a little confused. "No," she shook her head. "That tree is closer to the lake. I'll show it to you in the morning."

Dick moved closer to the tree for a better look as Kelly told him about the bizarre word. "Maybe we shouldn't have come here in the first place," he murmured.

"We had to!" Kelly said passionately. "How else could Heather solve the mystery for my grandparents?"

"I know this mystery means a lot to you, but someone could get hurt," Dick said.

"Kelly! Kelly!" her mother called into the woods. "What's going on out there?"

"Coming, Mrs. Fennimore!" Dick answered. "They're with me."

"Please don't make the group leave," Kelly begged.

"I'll have to think about that," he said firmly. "I can't have anyone's well-being jeopardized."

A few minutes later Heather, Kelly, and Mrs. Fennimore started walking back toward their tents. They were all deep in thought until they saw a dark shadow pass by them on the trail.

"What was that?" Kelly flashed her light on the path.

"It's a skunk!" Heather exclaimed hoarsely.

"Just ignore it," Mrs. Fennimore advised. "It'll go away."

But it didn't. The striped animal had come from the woods near the guys' tents and was prowling around for a quieter place to rest. Then it saw the women coming toward it. Deciding this was too much to take, the skunk lifted its tail and sprayed them with its noxious vapor!

4

Sizing Up the Scheme

Let's go down to the stream and wash ourselves off," Mrs. Fennimore instructed in her no-nonsense way. "I think I've got some soap in one of my pockets."

"We need more than soap and water to get rid of this awful smell," Kelly groaned.

"I've heard that tomato juice works wonders." Heather gagged on the sickening odor.

"We don't have tomato juice, and we can't get back to the camp tonight," Mrs. Fennimore said firmly before she began coughing, too.

She took them to the nearest stream, and they all jumped into the frigid water. They tried frantically to scrub away the horrible scent of skunk from their skin, hair, and clothes. It didn't work.

"I think we're going to have to sleep away from the others tonight," Heather said.

"I think you're right," Mrs. Fennimore agreed. "We can pull our tents down and set them up far enough away so the girls don't get totally grossed out."

"I feel like a leper," Kelly stated flatly as they went back to the girls' camp.

Everyone rushed to meet them, but quickly backed away as they sniffed skunk fumes.

"What is that awful smell?" Mrs. Lynch said as they approached.

"Ew!" Katie yelled.

"We got skunked," Heather stated. "We came back for our tents so you don't have to put up with us."

"Is that what happened at the guys' camp?" Katie asked them, breathing into her sleeve for some relief.

Once the female campers had heard all about the snake incident, they quickly retreated to their tents. Heather and her two companions endured a restless night, and in the morning, they prayed for Woodie to show up early. When he finally arrived, everyone begged him just to dump the supplies and take the skunked campers back to the lodge before he did another thing.

"You guys are ripe!" Mr. Fennimore teased.

"Don't I know it," his wife sighed. "I can hardly stand myself."

Before going back to the lodge, Heather took Jenn aside. "I'm going to try to stay with you today," she said. "I want to check out Sarah Cooper, and I have some questions for Kelly's grandparents."

"Phew!" Jenn held her nose. "I'd rather stay out here than hang around you today."

"Don't worry," Heather laughed, "I'll be all cleaned up by then."

An hour later Heather found herself at the lodge in a bathtub full of tomato juice. Kelly's grandmother had taken Heather to Sarah's rooms, Kelly to Woodie's, and Mrs. Fennimore to her quarters at the lodge.

"I can get you started, but you'll have to finish the job," the elderly woman stated. "I'm expecting company soon. I'll take your clothes with me. I'm afraid we'll have to burn them."

"What about my jacket and boots?"

"It's a shame, but you'll never get that smell out of them. I'll bring you some of Kelly's things," she said. "I think she's bigger than you, though. Jenn, come help me find something for Heather to wear."

"No problem," she said, hurrying toward the door. Jenn was eager to get away from the acrid scent that now filled Sarah's apartment.

"I guess I'll have to ask my parents to bring another coat and some boots to me," Heather sighed. *Mom and Dad are not going to be pleased,* she thought, remembering how much they had spent on her new parka.

As Kelly's grandmother and Jenn left with her things, Heather lowered herself into the thick red juice. It was the ickiest bath she had ever taken, but she had never welcomed one as much in her whole life either.

It wasn't until eleven o'clock that Heather was de-skunked enough to re-enter society.

"I'm still not what you'd call squeaky clean," she complained.

"No, but the smell is at least bearable," Jenn encouraged her. "Let's see how Kelly's doing."

Just as they opened the door to leave, the girls found Kelly on the other side getting ready to knock. She was fully dressed, but her hair was wet. "Can I borrow someone's blow dryer?" she asked. "Mom's using hers."

"I didn't bring one," Jenn said.

"I used Sarah's," Heather mentioned.

"Then I will, too." Kelly noticed the clothes Heather was wearing. "I think your outfit's a bit large," she smiled, beginning to see the humor in their situation.

"It's sure better than nothing!" Heather laughed.

While Kelly styled her short, dark hair, Heather discussed the previous night's events with Jenn.

"So, who do you think wrote that word on the tree and threw the snake at Dick?" the redhead asked afterward.

"It's just a guess, but I think someone wanted to scare Dick enough to get him to cancel the rest of the backpacking trip," Heather said.

"Why Dick?" Kelly asked over the roaring dryer.

"Because he's in charge."

"Why make him want to leave?" Jenn inquired.

"Maybe someone knows I'm trying to solve the mystery," Heather surmised. "Kelly, did you tell anyone I was going to try to find out what's going on at Camp Mohican?" she called into the bathroom.

"Yes," she said. "But only my grandparents, Sarah, and Woodie."

"Anyone else?" Heather asked.

"Come to think of it, a list of campers and the camp itinerary were posted on the bulletin board outside the lodge," Kelly said.

"So anyone could have used *chominiska* to let an accomplice know where Dick would be sleeping, right?" Kelly asked.

"Exactly," Heather said. She had a lot to tell her best friend. "Wait 'til you hear what happened last night!" she told Jenn. Heather filled her in on the snake incident and how they had discovered *chominiska* written on a tree. "I think that word alerted someone that the guys, and especially Dick, would be camping near there," Heather said. After a momentary pause she asked, "Kelly, what can you tell me about Woodie?"

"Well, first of all, I've always like him," she said, perching on the corner of Sarah's sleeper sofa in the living room. "His real name is Frank Wood. He's about seventy. He's a widower, and he started working at Mohican four years ago, after he had retired, and his wife had died. He really loves this place, so much that he's been working since August without pay."

"He has?" Heather asked. "Why?"

"Actually Sarah's been working for nothing, too, because my grandparents are so broke. Both of them have insisted on staying, though."

Heather frowned thoughtfully. "Is it dedication that's keeping them here, or something else entirely?"

"That, I don't know," Kelly admitted. "Let's just say I'm

more likely to question Sarah's motives than Woodie's. He's a great guy, even though he talks a little too much."

"Especially about the war!" Jenn rolled her eyes. "He never shuts up."

"Maybe I can dig up more information by hanging around here today," Heather said. "But first, I've got to call my parents and ask them to bring some outdoor clothes for me."

As they went to the phone on the lower level, she noticed that the Fennimores had company. Kelly's grandparents sat talking with four people: Sarah, an elderly woman, a man in his mid-twenties, and a middle-aged man wearing a real-estate badge.

"What is that odor?" The older woman turned up her nose.

"I'm afraid a skunk sprayed my daughter-in-law, granddaughter, and her friend," Kelly's grandmother grinned sheepishly. "What can I do for you, Kelly?" she asked, her voice implying that the sooner the three teenagers left, the better.

As Mrs. Fennimore spoke, Sarah shot an annoyed look at Heather and her friends. The young man with her scowled too. Then he quickly smiled charmingly at the elderly woman to his right.

"Heather needs to call her parents and ask them to bring more clothes," Kelly said. "I told her to use the phone down here."

"Well, all right," Kelly's grandmother conceded. She and her husband both seemed anxious to be rid of the girls.

Kelly took her friends behind the front desk that was fifteen feet from her grandparents and their guests. As Heather punched out her home number on the phone, she noticed that Sarah and the young man sat very close to one another. *He looks familiar,* she thought. *Oh, yeah! There's a picture of him in Sarah's living room. He must be her boyfriend.*

The young man sat there as if he owned the world, laughing and talking expansively. He called the elderly woman "Grandmother." No one else in their group looked at all happy, though Sarah was sure trying to do so.

"Hello, you've reached the Reeds," said the answering machine at Heather's house. At first Heather felt upset, thinking her parents were probably not at home, but then she had an inspiration. *Maybe they really can't come to the phone right now,* she thought. *I'll leave a message, and that will give me an excuse to wait here for them to call me back. I could learn a lot about what's going on around here!*

"Hi, Mom. Hi, Dad," she spoke into the receiver. "I'm calling from Camp Mohican. Last night on the trail a skunk sprayed me, Kelly, and her mom, and I need more backpacking clothes. Please call as soon as you get in. The number here is 717-555-1221. Thanks. Bye!"

"They're not in?" Kelly asked.

"No. Can we stay here, though? Maybe they'll be back soon, and I hate to miss their call," Heather said.

"I bet there's other stuff you don't want to miss," Jenn whispered.

Heather grinned at her as Kelly invited them to have a seat on some stools behind the front desk. Jenn started chattering about school and clothes, but Heather only half-listened. Instead she strained to hear what was going on with the Fennimores. A few minutes later, Kelly's mother came downstairs and asked what they were doing behind the desk. After Heather explained, Arlene Fennimore joined her parents and their visitors.

While Heather waited for her parents to call back, she learned an amazing thing. As she suspected, the young man with Sarah was her boyfriend. His name was Drew Hayward, and he was the person buying Camp Mohican!

"Of course, it's going to take mega-bucks to start a ski resort," he said, "but Grandmother will be helping me get on my feet. I would appreciate your coming down on the price, considering how I'll be struggling to rebuild this place's damaged reputation."

Heather watched Sarah Cooper as she listened to Drew and the Fennimores haggle over the price. *I wonder why she looks so miserable about it?* Heather thought. *Shouldn't this be good news for her as well?*

Suddenly the telephone rang, and Kelly answered it. "It's your mother," she told Heather.

"Heather, dear, are you all right?" Mrs. Reed asked.

"I am now," she replied, "although I still stink."

"We were on our way to the mall, but I forgot my purse. When I came into the kitchen, I saw the light flashing on the answering machine and listened to your message," Heather's mother explained. "Now I'm glad I was forgetful! What clothes do you need?"

Heather told her what to bring and apologized for the inconvenience.

"Don't worry about it," she commented. "It's the skunk who should be apologizing."

"So, when are they coming?" Jenn asked when Heather hung up the phone.

"They should be here just after lunch," she said.

"I think we'd better leave," Kelly stated, catching her mother's stern look. "Let's go for a walk. You can use my grandmother's jacket, Heather."

Heather thanked the Fennimores for letting her use the phone and went outside with Kelly and Jenn. They walked into a grove of blazing red maple trees and sat on a huge rock, discussing the news about Drew Hayward's ski resort.

"So that's who's buying Camp Mohican," Kelly shook her head. "I had no idea."

"Do you know Sarah's boyfriend?" Heather asked.

"Not very well, although he hung around a lot this summer. He always acts so cocky."

"Do you think they might have done all those mean things last summer to bring your grandparents to the point where they wanted to sell the place?" Jenn asked.

Kelly inhaled deeply, then said, "I guess it's possible."

"This area would make a great ski resort," Heather commented.

"Especially with a new interstate that had an exit right here," Jenn added.

Suddenly they heard voices. Heather motioned for her friends to keep silent, and she pointed silently toward

Sarah and Drew, who had come outside holding hands. The teenagers retreated behind the rock and waited for the couple to pass.

"My brother's giving me a hard time again," they heard Sarah complain.

"Duncan's just jealous that we beat him to the punch," Drew retorted. "What a great place Ski Mohican is going to be! The elevation will be the best for skiing in the Poconos. We'll make a fortune, Sarah, especially since I talked the Fennimores down so much on the price." He laughed viciously. "I think they'd take confederate money to get rid of the place now."

"I don't think my brother's jealous," Sarah protested.

"Face it, sweetheart," Drew said sarcastically, "he doesn't want to get stuck behind that desk for the rest of his life. He's told me as much." Her boyfriend paused and said in a sing-song voice, "Hey, he can always change his mind."

"He likes his job," Sarah defended meekly. She seemed afraid of Drew.

"Don't worry so much!" he growled.

"What about that snoopy girl?" Sarah asked.

Drew hit the palm of his left hand with his fist. "I'll take care of her!" he answered.

5

Taken for a Ride

The teenagers stared at each other in amazement. They now had proof of a plot to get the Fennimores to sell Camp Mohican! They also knew beyond any doubt that this couple was deeply involved. Sarah appeared to be having second thoughts, however.

"This part of it just makes me uneasy, Drew," she said, appearing to be on the edge of tears. "I don't want anyone getting hurt."

He draped an arm about her shoulders. "Believe me, sweetie, you'll forget all about your moral misgivings when you see the sports car I'm going to buy for you. Just picture yourself pulling that beauty into the spot with your name—correction, our name—on it," he said smoothly. "You'll be the envy of everyone at Ski Mohican. Not only that, but you'll be wearing this."

Drew pulled a jeweler's box out of his coat pocket, and Sarah opened it eagerly. "Drew!" she exclaimed. "It's enormous."

"Merely two carats," he bragged. "Allow me." He

slipped the engagement ring onto her finger and asked, "Will you marry me, Sarah?"

"Oh, yes!" she beamed.

Drew kissed her and said, "That's more like it! Believe me, I'll make you the happiest, richest snow queen this side of the Rockies. Now, let's get going. I want to tell Hawk the good news." He rubbed his hands together like a child. "I just knew Grandmother would sign for me. I wouldn't have gotten my hands on any of her money until she croaked, if I hadn't gotten her to 'invest' in Ski Mohican."

Sarah looked forlorn because Drew's big news was about the ski area, not their engagement. "I'm coming," she sulked. "Besides, I smell a skunk."

Although she was serious, Drew burst out laughing. He took her hand and strutted over to his white sports car where he placed a call on his cellular phone. He was too far away for Heather and her friends to listen in, but they could see that Drew looked mighty pleased with himself.

"Heather, do you think that mountain boy might be this Hawk person?" Kelly asked.

Her friend raised her eyebrows. "I was wondering the same thing. We have so little time and so much to find out," she sighed. "We're really going to have to be on our toes around here."

"Speaking of toes," Jenn said, pointing to her feet. "Can we please get up now? I can't tell if mine are asleep or frost-bitten."

"Sure," Heather laughed, noticing that the suspects had gone back inside the lodge.

Kelly made a suggestion. "Let's go down to the lake. It's very pretty, and we'll have more privacy."

"Good idea," Heather approved. "Maybe we'll air out a bit."

Jenn laughed. "I sure hope so."

As they walked toward the lake Heather said, "I think Drew's the ringleader in a conspiracy against the Fennimores."

"Yeah, and he's using Sarah and this Hawk person to get the camp," Jenn added.

"Woodie could easily be supplying information to them about us backpackers," Heather went on. "You know, Kelly, this also has me wondering about Duncan Cooper, Sarah's brother. From what you told me, I thought he might have been trying to scare away your folks so he could buy the camp. Now I'm not so sure."

"I see what you mean," Jenn nodded. "From what Sarah said, he's not too happy about this sale. Of course, it could be because he wanted the camp, and Drew got there first."

"Jenn, I'm going to need your help." Heather's eyes glowed with excitement.

"What do you want me to do?" She seemed hesitant. Jenn had gotten into some dangerous situations helping her friend solve mysteries.

"Watch Sarah closely. Look for any clues in her

apartment that might help us identify Hawk or the word *chominiska.*"

Jenn didn't think that sounded too hard. "Sure."

Heather suddenly snapped her fingers. "Better yet! You're stuck with me and Kelly until we make the supply run this afternoon or my parents come. We can look over Sarah's apartment together. Do you think she'll be away for a while?"

"She's usually not there much," Kelly said.

"I can help a little, but I need to work in the kitchen this afternoon. Your grandmother asked me to prepare salads and dessert for tonight," Jenn remarked to Kelly.

"When?" asked Heather.

"After lunch."

"I can help, too," Heather offered. "That'll give me the chance to question her about the mystery. Let's go back soon so we can start looking for clues."

When they returned to the lodge a half hour later, the reception room was empty. The teenagers went upstairs to Sarah's cluttered apartment, relieved to find that she was not there.

"I'm especially looking for any photographs that might identify Hawk and anything related to that word, *chominiska,* or the sale of Camp Mohican," Heather stated.

They quickly found some items of interest, including several pictures of Drew Hayward. In one of them he was at a ski resort looking tanned and fit. Standing next to him was a huge man with curly hair and a beard.

"I bet they worked together," Jenn pointed out.

"They're wearing uniforms from the Snow Queen ski area."

"That's the most popular resort in the Poconos," her friend murmured. "Kelly, do you know anything about Drew and his work?"

"No," she said. "Sarah never talks about him, and when he came around this summer, he usually avoided me."

"Where's the phone? I can call from here since it'll be local."

"Over there." Kelly pointed to the object that hung on Sarah's kitchen wall.

"I'm going to call Snow Queen and ask whether Drew Hayward works there," Heather said. "Maybe I can also find out who that other guy in the picture is."

"Good idea!" Jenn and Kelly approved.

When they could not find a phone book, Heather called directory assistance. Several minutes later she found herself talking to Snow Queen's personnel director, Maggie Fitzgerald.

"Yes, Drew Hayward worked here last year," she retorted.

"Do you mean he doesn't anymore?" Heather wasn't sure how much Ms. Fitzgerald would reveal.

"If you're interested in him, I'd suggest you forget it! He's a real charmer with those ski lessons he gives, but that's all he's good for," she advised. "Him and his buddy, John Hawk. I ended up firing both of them. Avoid them if you know what's good for you."

John Hawk! Heather thought. "Could you tell me if this Hawk guy is about Drew's age?" she asked.

"Yep. Cut from the same cloth those two are, except Hawk's not good-looking. It's all that hair. Listen, honey, I gotta go. My other line is ringing. Just remember, he's no good."

Heather thanked her and hung up. "Listen to this!"

"What happened? What's this about Hawk?" Jenn's eyes were practically popping out.

Heather repeated Maggie Fitzgerald's end of the conversation. "That hairy guy in the picture must be John Hawk," she showed them.

"So Hawk isn't the mountain boy?" Kelly asked.

"No," Heather shook her head. "I wonder who he is and what his role is in the plot?"

"From the way you described him, Kelly, he sounds like some wacko," Jenn shivered.

"He could be."

For the next fifteen minutes, the teenagers did a surface check of the apartment for any clues related to the mystery word, *chominiska*. They were careful not to delve into Sarah's private things.

"Girls!" Mrs. Fennimore called up the stairs, interrupting their probe. "It's time for lunch."

"Coming!" Kelly hollered. "I hope our lingering scent of skunk doesn't ruin everyone's appetites," she giggled.

"Not mine," Jenn announced. "I'm famished."

When they reached the Fennimore's private dining room next to the kitchen, they saw Kelly's mother and grandparents and Woodie sitting at the long walnut table.

"Sarah won't be joining us," Mrs. Fennimore announced.

She didn't provide a reason for the athletic director's absence, but Heather assumed it had something to do with the sale of the camp. The teenager considered this an opportune time to ask questions about Mohican's troubles. At first, the Fennimores answered reluctantly. As they finished their soup and sandwiches, then feasted on a delicious cranberry-apple pie, the elder Mrs. Fennimore's tongue loosened. Only her daughter-in-law remained tight-lipped and looked uncomfortable.

"I'm glad we were able to sell the place," Kelly's grandmother said, a tinge of sadness in her voice. "After all the bad publicity we had, I wasn't sure we could."

"That's for sure," Woodie muttered, forking another piece of the pie.

"Are you sorry it will become a ski resort?" Heather asked.

The older Mrs. Fennimore shrugged. Her quiet husband avoided Heather's glance. "I guess that's all right with me. Drew Hayward, that's Sarah's boyfriend, is a capable young man, and Sarah's very energetic. I'm sure they'll do well."

Mr. Fennimore coughed, and Heather thought he might be making a statement. His wife picked right up on it.

"My husband hasn't been too impressed with Sarah's work this summer, but I'm just glad she stayed on. She and Woodie. What would we do without you?" she asked the handyman fondly.

He smiled broadly. "Now don't fuss. I do what I have to."

And do you do it for yourself, them, or Drew? Heather wondered.

Neither Kelly's grandparents nor her mother believed there had been a conspiracy to force them into selling the camp.

"It was just bad luck," Mr. Fennimore muttered.

"I'd say you were snake bit," Woodie put in. "Sometimes your luck just runs the other way."

Heather could understand why the Fennimores felt so sad, although she wished they didn't act so defeated. But she wasn't sure about Woodie. *Saying they simply had bad luck would certainly throw any suspicion off him,* she concluded.

When the Reeds showed up right after lunch, Heather was overjoyed to get a fresh supply of outdoor gear. They spent the rest of the afternoon walking around the camp grounds.

"So," her dad asked, "have you run into any mysteries up here?"

"Actually I have," she remarked. Heather told her parents most of what had happened.

"Just be careful," Mrs. Reed cautioned. She always worried about her daughter's exploits.

At three-thirty it was time for Woodie to pack up the Bronco and head to the trail with the campers' food and tents. Since there was no room for the supplies and the extra passengers, however, Mr. and Mrs. Reed offered to take everything in their sizable minivan. When they arrived at the rendezvous site a half hour later, Pete and Evan were waving wildly at them. Mr. Reed quickly brought the vehicle to a halt, and they all jumped out to find out what was going on.

"We've got to get Catherine to the hospital!" Evan exclaimed.

6

Emergency!

W hat happened?" Heather cried out.

"A bunch of us stopped to look at a really neat hollowed-out tree," Evan said quickly, "and a swarm of bees flew at us."

"Five people got stung," Pete continued, "but Catherine Nitzel's breathing really hard."

"She must be allergic," Mrs. Reed, a pediatrician, assessed. Turning to her husband, she asked, "Honey, would you get my black bag in the minivan?"

Mr. Reed nodded and hurried to get the medical kit.

Immediately Woodie began unloading tents and supplies from the vehicle to make way for Catherine. "You fellas go back for the girl," he instructed. "Jenn and Heather, you can give me a hand here."

Less than ten minutes later a group arrived carrying Catherine in her sleeping bag. Dr. Reed had given her an injection of adrenaline, but she said the teenager required further treatment. As Heather lifted the last box of food from the back seat, she saw how Catherine's dark skin had swelled ominously. The girl was still breathing in short gasps.

"Put her in the back seat," Dick Walker ordered.

Evan, Mr. Fennimore, and Bill lifted Catherine onto the back seat of the minivan. Then Bill slipped in beside her and Mrs. Reed sat on her other side. Mrs. Fennimore was in the first row behind the driver.

"Shouldn't she be lying flat?" Jenn asked, leaning into the van.

Bill shook his head decisively as he clung to his girlfriend's hand. "She can't breathe as well in that position."

"I'll be happy to drive," Woodie told Mr. Reed. "I know where the hospital is and the fastest way to it."

Heather's dad handed Woodie the keys and got into the passenger seat.

"Heather and Jenn, too," Catherine rasped.

Her friends scooted into the cargo area, eager to be of help.

"See you later," Evan slammed the door behind them.

"Bye," Heather waved. "Pray for us."

Within minutes they were on the main road. Mrs. Reed called the hospital on her car phone and explained the situation as Woodie drove faster than the law allowed.

"I know the cops around here," he boasted as Catherine's wheezing increased. "If we get stopped, I'll tell them what happened. More than likely they'll escort us to the hospital."

I wonder whether knowing the police has helped him get away with other things? Heather asked herself. There was just something about him that she didn't trust.

Before they knew it, Woodie pulled into Pocono Central Hospital's emergency room driveway. Two white-coated orderlies flew through the double doors with a gurney.

"Is this the bee sting victim?" they asked.

"Yes," Mrs. Reed stated as the attendants put Catherine on the rolling stretcher.

They wheeled the girl straight to the emergency room where Mrs. Reed connected with the doctor on duty.

"Please call her parents," Mrs. Reed told Heather and her friends before disappearing behind the door.

While Woodie and Mrs. Fennimore went to the reception area to fill out the necessary papers, Heather, her dad, Bill, and Jenn found a pay phone in the lobby. Catherine's parents were naturally upset and said they wanted to come. After Mr. Reed gave them directions from Kirby, the Nitzels said they would be there as soon as they could.

Lacking for more to do, the foursome returned to the crowded waiting room where Bill retold the story of Catherine's bee sting. Although he had already gone through the details twice, Bill needed to repeat it. Mrs. Fennimore and Woodie joined them a half hour later.

"Any news?" Woodie asked hopefully.

"Not yet," Heather shook her head.

"I hope she's going to be okay," Mrs. Fennimore worried.

An hour-and-a-half after they had arrived, Mrs. Reed finally emerged with the other doctor.

"How is she?" Heather demanded, searching their faces for a clue.

"Catherine is resting comfortably now," said her mother.

"It's a good thing Dr. Reed gave Catherine that injection and that you got her here when you did," the male physician spoke. "If we had seen her just ten minutes later, she might not have made it."

"Thank God," Bill exhaled sharply, and Mr. Reed clapped a supportive hand on his shoulder.

"Where are the girl's parents?" the doctor on call asked.

"They're on the way," said Heather.

"I'll keep her in the ER until they get here, then," he decided. "How long do you think that will be?"

"Maybe just an hour more," Heather said. "Are you going to admit Catherine?"

Mrs. Reed shook her head. "That won't be necessary, but I don't think she should go backpacking again any time soon."

It was well past everyone's suppertime when the Nitzels came running through the emergency room entrance. Mrs. Reed took them right to see their daughter as she assured them that Catherine was all right. After they had seen the girl and talked to the doctor, Mr. and Mrs. Nitzel accompanied the others to the hospital's snack bar for a light meal.

"Thank you for all you've done," they told everyone several times. "You saved her life."

Mrs. Fennimore was obviously relieved. "I thought you'd be furious that this happened."

"It was no one's fault," Mrs. Nitzel reassured her. "These things just happen."

Do they? Heather wondered. *Every weird thing at Camp Mohican seems to happen by cruel design.*

"We've decided to take Catherine home," her mother stated.

"I think that's a good idea," Mrs. Reed approved.

"May I go back with you?" Bill requested eagerly.

"What about your backpacking?" Mr. Nitzel asked.

"I'd rather be with Catherine."

"We'd be glad to take you, son," her dad smiled.

"I guess you'll have to bring my stuff home," Bill told Heather and Jenn. When they said they would, Bill added, "Tell anyone who might need it to feel free to use my tent and sleeping bag."

Everyone got to visit briefly with Catherine before they left the hospital. She assured them that she felt much better and was eager to get home. It was nearly nine o'clock.

Kelly's mother was tired and frustrated as Mr. Reed, who was now driving, pulled out of the hospital's parking lot. "What could possibly happen next?" she sighed.

7

Pinnacle of Doom

On the way back from the hospital, Heather decided to ask Mrs. Fennimore some questions about Camp Mohican's recent misfortunes. She was particularly interested in getting more information about Sarah Cooper's brother, Duncan. *I'm really going to watch my step,* she told herself. *Kelly's mom hates this subject.*

"I guess this sort of emergency happens a lot during the summer season," the teenager said, leaning forward on the very back seat. Woodie sat in the first row with Mrs. Fennimore, and Jenn was next to Heather.

"Hopefully, this was the last one we'll ever have," Kelly's mother responded. Then she told the Reeds about Camp Mohican's sale.

"I think it's a terrible shame. I hate to see your family lose the place," Woodie told Arlene Fennimore.

"What can you do?" the woman shrugged.

"I'll bet it was a tough season," Heather said.

Woodie nodded. "It was."

"I guess it was even worse for Sarah. I mean with

her brother causing all that trouble over the new interstate."

"Has Kelly been filling your mind with her conspiracy theories?" Mrs. Fennimore asked Heather.

"No," she answered honestly.

Mr. and Mrs. Reed shook their heads as if to say, "What are we going to do with her?"

Although Kelly's mom was reluctant to say any more about the matter, Woodie couldn't wait to start.

"You know, that must be why Sarah's been so quiet," he remarked. "Her brother made enough noise around camp. Well, things are going to change for her now, anyway. I'm glad I'll be here to see it, too."

Heather was curious. "What do you mean?"

"Sarah and her boyfriend have asked me to work for them when they open their ski resort," he smiled.

Mrs. Fennimore regarded him strangely. "Well, good for you," she stated.

Heather wasn't sure whether she was genuinely happy for him or being sarcastic. *So Woodie's in tight with Sarah and Drew,* she thought. *That would give him a reason to try to sabotage the camp—if they promised to pay him well enough in the long-run.*

"I think Duncan Cooper was the reason for many of the Fennimores' problems," Woodie stated. "He and the Department of Transportation may be doing Sarah and Drew a favor by putting in that new interstate. However, I think the way he acted toward your husband's parents," he looked at Mrs. Fennimore, "upset Sarah. She really likes them."

"I guess our loss is at least someone else's gain," Mrs. Fennimore sighed. "Nothing good lasts forever anyway, right?"

Heather didn't think so. "I think it can," she said respectfully.

"Not here it can't," Mrs. Fennimore answered, her body stiffening.

"I hope everything works out well for all involved," Mr. Reed said kindly as he pulled into the main camp.

When everyone got out of the minivan, Mrs. Fennimore thanked the Reeds for their assistance. "I hate to leave so abruptly, but I have to tell my in-laws about the bee incident now."

"Yeah, and I'd better get to bed," Jenn yawned sleepily. She said good-night to everyone and headed for Sarah's apartment.

"I'll get Woodie to take you back to the trail, Heather," Mrs. Fennimore said. She looked around. "I wonder where he went?"

"We can take her there," Mrs. Reed said.

Kelly's mother was insistent. "That won't be necessary. You have a long trip back to Kirby—unless, of course, you'd prefer to stay here tonight."

"I'm afraid we can't," Mr. Reed said.

"Well, you go right ahead, then, and Woodie will take Heather to the trail. Just wait here," she told the girl.

After Mrs. Fennimore went to the lodge, Heather and her parents said good-bye.

"Thanks again for bringing my clothes."

"Just try to avoid the skunks, okay, Heather?" her dad joked.

They drove off down the dirt road to the main highway, and Heather waited impatiently for Woodie to return. *That's strange,* she thought. *Mrs. Fennimore said he would take me back. I wonder what happened to him.*

Twenty minutes later she decided to hike back using the main access road. *There's no use staying around here,* she reasoned. *It's not that far to walk anyway.* Heather flung her backpack over her shoulders and started down the two-mile stretch of road that would take her to the trail. Darkness had fallen, and although she had a good flashlight to illumine her way, Heather found that the road took on a different aspect on foot and at nighttime. For one thing, she didn't remember seeing the route branch off onto even smaller dirt roads. The first two were easy to ignore because they looked so small and indirect. The third, however, presented a problem as it loomed into view several feet before her. The main road forked, forcing Heather to decide.

As the teenager consulted her compass, she determined that the way back to the trail camp was to the right. She snapped the case shut, content that she was going the right way. The feeling didn't last. Suddenly Heather heard fallen leaves crunching under foot, but it wasn't *her* foot. The sound came from several feet away in the woods flanking the road.

It's probably just a raccoon or a squirrel, she told herself, but Heather's shallow breathing betrayed her fear.

When the footfalls from the woods matched hers step-for-step, and her pursuer breathed as loud as a bellows, Heather flashed her light into the trees. The other's steps continued at a slower pace, but the husky breathing quickened. *Where is it?* Heather thought. *And what is it?* Failing to find the creature in the woods, she aimed the light at the trail in front of her.

Oh no! she gasped, catching a glimpse of a big brown bear with nails like mini-bayonets. Although it looked hungry, it did not growl. *It's standing right in the way of where I need to go!* she thought wildly. *How will I ever get back to the trail?*

Heather knew she couldn't outrun a bear. She had also learned from a trail safety class that sudden movements provoke the animals. *I'll have to go down the path to the left,* she decided, *and trust I don't get hopelessly lost!*

Her pulse raced as she walked quickly in the direction of the other trail trying to look unafraid. Turning around, she hoped to find the bear moving away from her. Unfortunately it had decided to follow the teenager!

Lord, help me stay calm, Heather prayed.

She kept walking straight ahead, her heart thumping wildly in her chest. She flipped off the flashlight, hoping to confuse the bear on her whereabouts. The only problem was that she couldn't see where she was going. A few minutes later, Heather's right boot caught on a vine growing across the trail, and she fell with a loud *OOMPH!* As she went down, the teenager put out her hands to break the fall. *There was nothing in front of her!* Her flashlight had fallen from her pocket, but she didn't hear it hit the ground. It wasn't until several seconds later that she heard a weak "splash" below her. Wide-eyed with horror, Heather felt around and soon discovered that she was at the edge of a cliff! *This must be the Pinnacle that Dick told us about!* she realized.

Heather untangled her foot from the strong vine that had tripped her, thanking God for the fall. Another few steps, and she would have fallen to her death! Hearing the bear just twenty or so feet away, Heather scrambled to her feet and went to her right, careful to stay near the trees. She didn't know how long the Pinnacle was and didn't want another close encounter with it.

I hope I'll lose the bear in these trees, she thought. *I just wish I had my flashlight so I could see where I'm going.*

Heather had only gone a few feet when she suddenly bumped into something warm. *"OOMPH!"* she exclaimed again. As she backed away, the outline of a person came into sharper focus. It was the mountain boy, and he stood with his bow and arrow raised to shoot!

8

Between a Rock and a Hard Place

Heather was so scared she choked on her scream. As she watched the powerful bear move closer, she wondered which of the two would kill her, the beast or the boy?

The bear made the first move, lunging toward Heather with its giant claw. Just as quickly the mountain boy, shooting point blank, sent an arrow into the animal's upper left arm. Heather gaped in fascination as the bear gave a startled cry and disappeared into the trees.

How creepy! she trembled. *It sounded almost human.*

Her relief lasted only seconds. Saved from the bear, Heather now faced the strange mountain boy's weapon. As she turned to confront him, Heather became confused. He was gone!

Where in the world did he go so fast? She twirled around looking for him. She didn't even catch a passing glimpse, though. *If Kelly hadn't told me he existed, I might be tempted to think he was a figment of my imagination! I wonder if he could be one of Drew and Sarah's accomplices. But then after all, he* did *save my life.*

The teenager didn't spend any more time in reflection. Still weak from terror, she fled from the scene, carefully making her way back to her friends' campsite. She stayed at least ten feet from the Pinnacle's cliff. Heather got side-tracked a few times because she didn't have her flashlight to guide her. She did have a strong incentive to keep going, though—the bear might find her in the woods. She knew the animal wouldn't be in a good mood either. Fifteen minutes later Heather saw her group's campfire. As she entered the lighted area, her knees buckled.

"Heather!" Kelly screamed. "What's wrong?"

"Is Catherine okay?" Katie Lynch called out as several campers encircled Heather.

"Are you all right?" Evan asked.

"Give her a chance to catch her breath!" Dick Walker exclaimed, but he was just as eager as the rest to find out what had happened.

Sushmita handed Heather a cup of hot chocolate, and the petite teenager took it with trembling hands.

"Where's Bill?" Pete asked.

"Where's Woodie?" Mr. Fennimore demanded, expecting to see the handyman with Heather. He didn't think she should have come back alone.

Where's Woodie, indeed! Heather thought, sipping the foamy chocolate and feeling strengthened. "I don't know what happened to Woodie," she finally said. "He was supposed to drive me here, but we got separated at the lodge."

"I'll have a talk with him," Evan muttered angrily.

"Are you hurt, Heather?" Pete asked anxiously.

Heather had not planned to share her story with anyone but Dick, Kelly, Evan, and Pete. She had suffered such a scare, though, that the words flowed like a torrential downpour. When she finished telling them about the bear, Heather also filled them in on what had happened with Catherine.

"We should go back to the lodge," Mrs. Lynch stated. "What happened with Catherine and Heather means we shouldn't be here."

"Yes, let's go back," Katie begged Dick. "Too much stuff is going wrong out here."

Pete muttered, "What makes you think we'd be safe back there?"

"I think everyone is frightened," Sushmita said, "including myself."

One of the younger youth group members stood defiantly with her hands on her hips. "I've had enough of this camping junk."

"Me, too!" a guy agreed.

"My back hurts," someone else complained.

"My feet are covered with blisters," another guy moaned. "I can hardly walk."

"I got poison ivy—in this weather!" came another protest.

"This place gives me the creeps," another kid declared.

"Some of the gang just aren't into backpacking," Kelly told Dick and her father. The two men looked disappointed.

"As you can see, Heather, I'm facing mutiny," Dick grinned wryly, then added, "Everyone's so jumpy. Kelly's been telling them what went on here this summer."

"At least *they* listen to me," Kelly said moodily, overhearing his remark. She glared at him and her father.

Dick's face reddened. "Maybe we should go back to the lodge," he said, appealing to Mr. Fennimore and the Lynches.

"We could take a vote to see what everyone wants," Mr. Fennimore suggested.

"I think that's the best way to deal with this," Dick decided. "Okay. Those who want to complete the trip, raise your hands." Ten hands went up, mostly guys'. "And those of you who want to leave, raise your hands now." The rest of the hands went up, including Katie Lynch's and her parents'. "Okay, we'll split along those lines, then, especially since we've got parents in both groups. Do you think your wife will want to stay out here?" he asked Mr. Fennimore.

He nodded. "I'm almost certain she would."

"Good," said Dick. "Joe and Sue Lynch can send her back here when they return. Now, can the returning group stay in those dorms back at the main camp?"

Kelly's father nodded. "I think that's a good idea."

"Terrific." Dick whistled to get everyone's attention. "Since Woodie isn't here to help, everyone who wants to go back now will have to carry his own gear or stay out here one more night," Dick announced.

The thirteen in question said they would walk to the main camp now. They began packing up their things.

"What made you decide to leave the trail, Heather?" Evan asked.

She lowered her voice and told him, Pete, and Kelly. "This way I can keep an eye on some suspects at the main camp."

"What about you? Why are you leaving?" Heather asked her friends.

"I'm not about to let you solve the mystery by yourself," Evan laughed.

"I want to be where the excitement is," said Pete. He added slyly, "And it's usually with Heather and Jenn!"

"What about you, Kelly?" Heather inquired.

"I want to help you solve the mystery, too," she answered. "I . . ."

"Kelly," her father walked over to them. "I need you to stay out here where we still have beginners."

"But, Dad . . ."

"That's my final word."

As Mr. Fennimore walked away, Kelly bit her lower lip in frustration. "He and Mom just don't want me snooping around."

Heather felt sorry for her friend. "I wish you could come with us," she said, "but then we wouldn't have anyone keeping an eye on the trail."

Kelly's face broke into a smile. "You think so?"

"Sure."

"Then I'll stay."

When the teenagers and their chaperons returned to the camp, Heather noticed Woodie lingering on the edges of the group, trying to be helpful. Anger welled up in her, and she walked over to him boldly.

"Where were you?" she demanded.

"Where was I?" he asked, looking genuinely bewildered.

"Mrs. Fennimore asked you to take me back to the trail, but you never showed up, and I nearly got mauled by a bear!" Heather trembled.

Woodie's eyes nearly popped out. "Sarah came and told me you had changed your mind and would be staying at the lodge."

"Sarah?"

"Yes. Right after we returned from the hospital, Arlene Fennimore asked me to take you to the trail. I told her I had to get something from my room first. Then, on my way to get you, Sarah told me you had changed your mind and would be staying with her and Jenn," Woodie explained nervously. "I feel terrible about what happened. Are you all right?"

"Fine," Heather answered coolly. *I wonder just how terrible he feels,* she thought.

"Here, let me take your pack," Woodie offered.

"I can get it myself," she pulled it away.

"It's no problem," he insisted.

"Yes, it is. Leave me alone."

"What's going on?" Evan asked, walking over to them.

Woodie looked first at Heather, then at her friend.

"I think everything's okay now," she said.

A half hour later Heather sat on a spongy cot, rummaging through her pack and talking to Jenn. Mrs. Lynch was about to ask Jenn to go back to the lodge so they could get some rest when Kelly's mother appeared in the doorway.

"I heard about what happened with the bear," she told Heather. "Are you all right?"

"I'm fine," she reassured the anxious-looking woman.

"Thank God for that!" she sighed. Then Mrs. Fennimore said she had a favor to ask. "I wonder if you would mind running to the store for me, Jenn? I knocked on Woodie's door in the lodge, but he has already gone to bed. Sarah's on the phone, and I'm at my wit's end."

"What's wrong?" Jenn asked.

"With all the excitement about the sale today, my mother-in-law forgot to have a prescription refilled. She needs a pill tonight. Unfortunately my father-in-law's already in bed, and I have to get back to the trail. Could you and your friend, Evan, pick up the medicine for me?" she asked.

Jenn swung her legs over the side of the cot. "I'd be glad to."

"I feel funny letting you go like this, but my options are so limited," she said, handing her the medicine bottle. "The store closes in forty minutes."

"I'd like to go, too," Heather said.

"Are you sure you feel up to it?" the older woman asked.

"Sure."

"Well, suit yourself," Mrs. Fennimore shrugged.

She accompanied Heather and Jenn to the boys' dorm where she explained the situation to Mr. Lynch. Soon

Heather sat in the Bronco's passenger seat with Evan at the wheel and Pete and Jenn in the back. Pete had insisted on going, too.

"This old tank sure is getting a workout this weekend!" Evan exclaimed.

Suddenly the Bronco veered off the road. It bucked wildly as Evan fought to avoid hitting a telephone pole!

9

Bucking Bronco

W e're gonna crash!" Jenn screamed, bracing herself.

Pete threw his arms around her protectively, and Heather clung to the dashboard. Evan desperately swerved away from the pole, praying that he could avoid it. After bumping and grinding several feet, the Bronco thudded to a standstill at the side of the road. They had barely missed the telephone pole!

"Can I look now?" Jenn asked timidly. She started peeking, one finger at a time.

"I think so," Pete said, wiping his forehead with the back of his hand. "It looks like we're all in one piece. Man, Evan! What happened back there?"

"The tire blew." His hands shook on the wheel. "Heather, are you okay?"

She sighed heavily. "Physically, yes. Mentally, I'm a wreck. A bear, a mountain boy, and now this. What a day!"

"I'm sure sorry about this," Evan apologized.

"I think that was an expert piece of driving," she praised.

"Thanks." Although he blushed, Heather could tell he appreciated the compliment. "I'm going to look at that tire. The strangest thing is, I just got it a month ago."

Heather and the others also got out of the Bronco. They discovered that the right front tire had a deep gash in it.

"Look at this!" Heather exclaimed. The others drew closer and were astonished to find an arrowhead lodged in the tire.

"I think we'd better put on the spare and get out of here," Evan stated, looking around warily. "Someone did this to us on purpose. Pete, give me a hand."

"I'd like to investigate," Heather said.

"Now's not a good time," Evan cautioned. "We've got to hurry. Besides, whoever did this still may be waiting in the woods."

"Let's go, Heather," Jenn yanked at her friend's sleeve.

"I guess you're right," she conceded.

By the time the guys had fixed the tire, they had only minutes to get to the pharmacy before it closed. After getting the prescription refilled, the teenagers stopped by the scene of the accident on their way back to Camp Mohican.

"I want to search for footprints," Heather said, opening her door to get out and investigate.

"I'd rather not," Jenn said timidly.

"You can stay here and wait," Evan told her.

The redhead's hand was already on the door handle. "Uh, come to think of it, I'll go with you."

Heather and her friends took flashlights and walked carefully into the woods, looking for signs of the attacker. Almost immediately she saw man-sized footprints on the dusty ground.

"These are way too big to be the mountain boy's," she remarked to the other. "Let's look for the word, *chominiska*. Maybe that will come into play."

But it didn't.

"Look at these branches," Evan directed their attention to some broken tree limbs. "Looks like our assailant crashed through here in a hurry."

Heather examined them up closer. "They're snapped at a level that would be too high for the mountain boy. I'd say an adult sent that arrow into the tire."

"Let's get out of here," Jenn pleaded. "This place is creeping me right out."

On the way back to Camp Mohican, they discussed who could have ruptured their tire and why.

"I think either Woodie or Sarah could have done it," Pete reflected.

"It's possible," Heather said.

"So the mountain boy's out?" Evan asked.

"I think so. As I said, the footprints we found were adult-sized—large adult-sized to be exact—and those broken branches were too high for the boy."

"Might they have been too high for Sarah?" Jenn suggested.

"Hmm," Heather said. "She is pretty tall."

"So is Woodie," Jenn went on.

"Yeah, but those footprints were huge," Evan pointed out. "I doubt Sarah's feet are that big."

"She still could have been in on it, though," Pete stated.

A few silent minutes had passed when suddenly Heather cried out, "That's it!"

Jenn slapped her hand to her chest. "Heather, don't do that to me! You scared me half to death."

"Sorry," she apologized. "It's just that maybe someone wanted us to *think* the mountain boy had done it. I mean wouldn't we think so when we saw the arrowhead?"

"That makes sense," Pete reflected.

"So that would mean the mountain boy isn't in on the plot against Camp Mohican," Evan concluded.

"There could be another reason," Pete added.

"What's that?" asked Heather.

"Everyone who's in on the scheme might use bows and arrows as a kind of signature."

"Possibly," she hesitated. She paused for a moment then said, "The first thing I'd like to do is find out where Woodie and Sarah were when the tire blew."

When they returned to the lodge, the young people delivered the medicine to a grateful Mrs. Fennimore. They did not tell her what had happened with the Bronco.

"I can't thank you enough," the older woman said. "I was beginning to worry that you wouldn't get to the pharmacy in time. Why did you take so long?"

"We had a flat tire," Evan said quickly.

"Oh, too bad. I hated to put you out, but there was no one else."

After Mrs. Fennimore left them, Jenn led her friends to Woodie's apartment on the second floor. It was just down the hall from Sarah's.

"Mrs. Fennimore said Woodie had gone to bed for the night," Heather reminded them. "Maybe he only pretended to."

"He could have climbed out his window so no one would have seen him leave his room," Evan said.

"Let's take a look from the outside," Heather suggested.

They could see that Woodie's windows were shut tightly. Nor were there broken tree limbs, footprints, or a ladder to suggest that the handyman had sneaked out of his room through the window.

"He might never have gone to his room," Pete remarked. "Maybe he was just hanging around near our dorms waiting for an opportunity to skunk us."

"Please don't use that word," Heather groaned. They all laughed.

"Kelly's mother said Sarah was on the phone when she tried to find someone to go to the pharmacy," Evan proceeded. "She could have seen this as an opportunity to scare us off and alerted her boyfriend or Woodie about our late-night run."

"Or that Hawk guy," Heather added.

Jenn yawned and stretched. "I've had enough of this mystery for tonight. I'm going to bed. Wish me well with surly Sarah," she frowned.

"It is pretty late," Pete agreed. "They'll be worried about us back at the dorms."

They said good-night to Jenn and headed back to their new quarters.

"I hope we all have a restful night," Heather said softly at her door. She didn't want to wake anyone.

"See you in the morning!" the guys whispered.

Everyone in Heather's dorm was fast asleep, so she quietly removed her parka and mittens, then crawled into her sleeping bag. Sleep claimed her quickly, but it didn't last. Twenty minutes later, as she was dreaming that a bear was trying to break into the building, Heather awakened with a start. Something *was* scratching at the door!

10

Bad News and Bears

Heather scurried out of her sleeping bag as other sleepers awakened.

"What is that noise?" Sushmita asked nervously.

"I don't know," Heather responded. "Just stay put. I'm going to check it out."

She slipped into a pair of shoes as the scratching at the door continued. As the teenage detective moved stealthily toward the entrance, the intruder abruptly burst through the door and knocked her to the floor! As Heather fell, the intruder tripped over her, landing with a startled wail.

"I heard a noise!" Mrs. Lynch cried out, her voice heavy with sleep and confusion. Then she turned on the lights.

"It's me!" yelled Jenn as she raised her arms across her face to soften the punch Heather was about to deliver.

"Jenn!" she shouted. Heather began to tremble; she had come within inches of striking her best friend.

"What happened?" Mrs. Lynch demanded as the other girls exclaimed over the surprise visit. "Are you all right, Jenn?"

"My knee hurts a bit, but I'm okay," the redhead commented.

Heather helped her friend get up, and Mrs. Lynch took Jenn's pack and placed it on an empty cot. "What's this all about?" the woman demanded.

I'm wondering the same thing, Heather thought.

"Uh, I'm supposed to stay here now," Jenn muttered.

"Well, you think Mrs. Fennimore would have arranged this earlier," the chaperon huffed.

Heather knew something was up. As the other girls calmed down, she said, "Mrs. Lynch, I'd like to use the bathroom before we get back to bed." *I have a thousand things I want to ask Jenn,* she thought, glancing at her friend.

"I'll go with you," Jenn quickly agreed.

"Well, all right, but do hurry back. It's nearly midnight. Does anyone else need to go?" Mrs. Lynch asked the others.

Heather waited tensely for the answer. She hoped no one said they did. She got her wish, and they left the building. Jenn's flashlight cast weird shadows on the forest floor. Heather looked to her left and right, wondering if they were alone.

"I've got so much to tell you!" Jenn said.

"Was someone chasing you?" Heather asked.

"No. Let me take it from the top." She inhaled deeply as they walked briskly toward the rest rooms. "After you guys left, I went to Sarah's apartment," Jenn began. "I had just washed up and slipped into bed when she stormed in."

"So she had been out?" Heather inquired.

"Yup. Then the phone rang, and when Sarah picked it up, she put it on the speaker phone and started undressing for bed. I heard everything."

"What a break!" Heather exclaimed. "Who called?"

"Her brother, and he was not pleased."

"Oh, tell me everything!"

The two teenagers hurried into the cement building with its coarse spider webs and damp odor. Jenn spilled the rest of the story as a leaky faucet dripped in the background.

"Duncan really chewed Sarah out. He said she'd better reconsider her decision if she knew what was good for her."

"Did it sound like a threat?" Heather wanted to know.

"No," Jenn drew out the word. "It was more like, 'This isn't good for you.'"

"Did he say why?" her friend asked with a sneeze.

"God bless you," Jenn giggled. "No, he didn't, but Sarah went on a tirade. She said, 'You'd change your tune if I were doing this for you.'"

"Then what?"

"Duncan said, 'You'll live to regret it.'" Jenn seemed pleased with herself. "So, what do you think?"

"I think you did a great job!" Heather smiled warmly. Then she brooded quietly for a while, twisting a lock of her hair around a finger. Finally she asked, "So, how did you end up out here instead of staying with Sarah?"

"After she hung up on Duncan, Sarah started throwing

stuff around the room. Her toy polar bear beaned me, and it was like she realized for the first time that I was in her apartment and had heard everything," Jenn explained. "Then I noticed a slip of paper that had fallen to the floor during her fit. I picked it up and, guess what?"

"What?" Heather begged.

"It had that weird word written on it!"

"Chominiska?"

"That's the one!" Jenn grinned. "I handed the paper to Sarah and asked what it meant."

"Did she tell you?" Heather asked breathlessly.

"No. She grabbed it away from me and told me to get out of her apartment. That's why I came back here."

Jenn prattled on about packing in a hurry, but Heather only half-listened. When she didn't respond after a few minutes, Jenn waved her hand in front of her friend's face.

"Heather? Heather!"

"What?" she asked, startled.

"You were a million miles away. What gives?"

"I was thinking about Sarah. Is that all you can tell me?"

"I thought that was quite enough," her friend said defensively.

"You did a wonderful job, Jenn. I'm simply wondering if there's anything else you want to say before we go back. Mrs. Lynch will expect us to go straight to sleep, you know."

"There isn't." Then she sighed. "Those cots are so grim."

"I don't think you're a happy camper."

"You got that right!"

As they walked back, Heather was in a reflective mood. "I get the impression that Sarah may be having second thoughts about Drew buying Camp Mohican. Remember that conversation she had with him earlier today?"

"Yeah," Jenn agreed. "Her conscience may be bothering her."

"I want to watch her closely."

Her friend fell silent for a moment then said, "I hate these dark woods. I have the feeling someone's watching us."

Heather had the same spooky hunch. They were just fifty feet from the building when Heather heard a noise behind them.

"What's that?" Jenn clutched her arm.

"Just keep going," she advised. "Maybe it's an owl or something."

"Let's hurry!"

Jenn started running blindly toward the dorm, stumbling over tree stumps in her haste. Heather knew it was no owl when she heard their pursuer panting and grunting. The noise spooked Jenn so badly that she let out a blood-curdling scream.

"Run!" Heather yelled.

When they finally got to the door, Jenn scrambled inside first, pulling Heather after her. She, in turn, snapped the door shut.

"What in the world!" Mrs. Lynch was annoyed.

"A bear is after us!" Jenn shrieked.

"A bear!" the other girls screamed, fully awake.

Shrieks filled the dorm. Then voices drifted in from the guys' building several yards away. Heather wanted to go outside to see what was happening, but Mrs. Lynch insisted she stay put. Moments later someone pounded on the door.

"It's the bear!" Sushmita shouted.

"It's all right, ladies," Mr. Lynch called to them. "Come see your bear."

Everyone rushed to the door, jostling for a good look. Then Katie burst into nervous giggles. "It's only Pete Gubrio!" she exclaimed.

Jenn pushed closer and saw her friend standing self-consciously next to Mr. Lynch. When Pete caught Jenn's eye, he blushed.

"I'm sorry, everybody," he apologized. "I had trouble sleeping and was looking out the window when I saw Heather and Jenn walk by. I couldn't resist playing a joke on them."

"Honestly!" Mrs. Lynch huffed. "You should be sorry. C'mon, ladies. Go back to bed. It's late." She shooed them away from the door.

"Forgive me?" Pete asked Jenn and Heather before they left.

"I'll think about it," Jenn said coldly.

"You scared us half to death," Heather charged. Then she relaxed. "I'm sure we'll see the humor in it in the morning."

As she crawled back into bed, she heard Katie tell Sushmita, "We wouldn't have been so scared if there weren't real bears roaming around the camp."

"Go to sleep, girls," Mrs. Lynch told them as she turned off the lights. "Everything's all right now."

Heather still thought everything was all wrong.

On Saturday morning she lay in her sleeping bag, mentally reviewing the events of the previous night. *I hope something major happens today,* she concluded. *We go home tomorrow, and if I don't solve this mystery, the Fennimores will lose Camp Mohican.*

Except for Heather and Jenn, the other girls had already gone to the showers. Mrs. Lynch told them to hurry. "I don't want you to miss breakfast," she stated. "It's getting late."

The two friends got up and hastened to the showers, carrying their towels and soap. About halfway there, Heather caught a whiff of something sweet. Then she saw a figure standing near a tree to the right.

"Jenn," she whispered, slowing down. "Look over there."

Her friend's blue eyes widened. "Who is that?"

"Let's get closer." They walked quietly, parting some branches of a red maple tree for a better look.

"It's Woodie!" Heather whispered with excitement. "And look what he's doing!"

11

Up a Creek

He's smearing honey on that tree!" Jenn exclaimed.

Dropping her soap and towel, Heather boldly confronted Woodie. "What on earth are you doing?"

"Heather!" he exclaimed. Then he shook his head. "I'm sick and tired of this confounded bear! I'll catch the beast if no one else will. I won't have things spoiled for Sarah, too."

She and Jenn gaped at each other. *Have I been wrong about him?* Heather wondered. *It seems like he's only trying to help.*

"So you're going to attract the bear with honey?" she asked.

"Darn tootin'," Woodie answered proudly. "You see, during the second World War we had to be on the lookout for predators."

Jenn rolled her eyes as Woodie began to tell another war story. Heather listened attentively. She had a feeling that the handyman's part in the mystery was about to be made known.

"We used all sorts of decoys to trap the critters," Woodie continued. "It was best to bring them into the open, rather than wait for them to make the first move. I know someone pulled a fast one on you last night, but there still is a real bear roaming around here." Then he remembered something else. "I also heard about what happened with the Bronco last night. I hope you're both okay."

"We are," Heather said. "How'd you find out?"

"Sarah told me this morning."

Sarah! Heather thought.

"I would've been happy to go to the pharmacy for Mrs. Fennimore, but I was so bushed that I went to bed extra early last night. She didn't want to wake me up neither." Woodie hung his head. "I sure have let you down, Heather. First the mix-up over getting you back to the trail, then the flat tire. Please forgive me."

She was beginning to warm up to Woodie. "Certainly," Heather answered. "And I'm sorry for confronting you like I just did. I usually behave more respectfully than that."

Woodie's grin brightened his downcast face, and they shook hands. "Do you mind?" He gestured toward the tree and his work.

"Not at all," Heather smiled.

"Me neither," Jenn echoed, approving the goodwill between them.

As Woodie finished his bear trap, the teenagers headed toward the showers.

"I think he's okay after all," Jenn said.

"I think so, too," Heather nodded. "He really does seem to care about the Fennimores, and he likes feeling needed here."

"It sure looks that way. You know, Heather," Jenn said repentently, "I haven't been very respectful toward him myself. I mean, 'World War Woodie' and all that. My grandfather was in the war, and he tells stories, too. Mom tells us kids to listen, but we usually just laugh." She paused and smiled. "From now on, I'm going to try harder."

"I think that's a nice idea," Heather said as they neared the showers. A moment later she groaned. "Oh, no!"

"What!" Jenn was understandably jumpy.

"I dropped my soap and towel by the trees when we first saw Woodie, and I never bothered to pick them up. You go on ahead, Jenn. I'll catch up with you."

"Okay, but hurry. We'll really be late for breakfast now!" Heather knew right where the spot was and quickly returned to it. On the way she said good morning to other campers as they went to breakfast at the lodge's rustic dining hall.

"Are you coming?" asked one guy as they passed.

"I'll be there as soon as I can," she promised.

Twenty minutes later Heather arrived late for the morning meal and announcements. Afterward they asked Evan and Pete to fill them in.

"So, what's on the schedule?" Jenn asked. "The mall, maybe? A nice shopping spree? More practical jokes?"

Pete grinned. He was glad to know Jenn wasn't still

furious with him. "No mall," he said. "Mr. Lynch wants us to take a canoe trip out to the trail campers."

"We're supposed to bring sandwiches and have lunch with them," Evan continued. "Since we can't paddle upstream when we're finished, we'll hike back, and Woodie will go after the canoes."

"Sounds great!" Heather said. "Maybe the culprits have struck on the trail again, and Kelly can tell us all about it."

"Oh, joy," Jenn moaned. "I just love canoes."

"That's right, you always get seasick," Heather teased.

"Are you willing to try?" Pete asked hopefully. "This stream should be pretty gentle."

"Well, I guess so." Jenn didn't mind spending time with Pete.

Heather lowered her voice so no one could overhear her. "Listen, guys, please be on the alert for anything out of the ordinary when we get there."

Just then Sarah Cooper walked by and smiled in their direction.

"Like that," Jenn snorted. "I've never seen her smile before, especially not at me."

"That's exactly the kind of thing to look for," Heather commented. "I wonder what brought that on?"

Shortly afterward, they followed the Lynches and Sarah to the lakefront where Woodie was pulling red canoes out of a boathouse. The sun shone brilliantly, and migrating Canadian geese honked greetings as they passed overhead. Sarah asked everyone to get close so they would hear her instructions.

"This lake connects with the stream that will lead us to the campers," she explained. "How many of you can operate a canoe?"

A few people raised their hands, including Heather.

"I need everyone who can to pair up with someone who can't."

For the next few minutes Sarah organized everyone into couples. Since Heather and Evan knew how to use a canoe, they didn't get to ride together. In the end, Heather was left without a partner.

Sarah outfitted each of the seven couples with a canoe, paddles, and safety vests. When she came to Heather, she asked, "Are you sure you can handle this?"

Heather nodded. "Quite sure."

"Good." Then she shouted so everyone would hear. "We'll paddle down past the swimming area and along that grove of hemlock trees," she pointed. "Just past them you'll see the stream. Let's be extra careful not to bump into each other."

"Is the stream rough?" Jenn asked uneasily.

"No, except for one of the bends," Sarah remarked. "We'll have to portage—or carry—the canoes around it. It's got a powerful current, and it's often hard to tell you're in trouble until it's too late. If you follow me, you'll be okay."

"Wonderful," Jenn muttered sarcastically.

Sarah climbed into her boat with Sushmita as her passenger, and led the group onto the shimmery lake. As she told each rower where he or she should be,

Heather found herself at the rear of the procession. *This canoe is so sluggish,* she thought in frustration. Her feet also got wet from a slightly leaky bottom, but it was more of a nuisance than a problem. As Sarah continued to bark directions at the others, Heather fell farther behind.

About twenty minutes into the excursion, she realized with a start that she had drifted far from the others. The stream was no longer placid. It began to foam and roar in the near distance, suggesting rough water ahead.

"Now, how did I lose them?" Heather asked herself.

She steered hard to hug the shore line, but the rough water kept pulling her toward the middle of the turbulent stream. Then she saw the jagged rocks a few feet ahead. The mighty torrent swept her toward them, and before she knew it, the bottom of the canoe scraped hard against one. It made an unearthly groan, and Heather gave a cry as she saw the bottom of the craft fill rapidly with swirling water.

As the water swept her and the disabled boat further out of control, Heather panicked. Twenty feet ahead of her, a waterfall swooped over a fifteen-foot drop. She paddled frantically to avoid the danger zone, but her strength was running out, and the water's force was relentless.

"God, help me!" she cried as the canoe plunged over the falls.

12

Wipeout!

Heather closed her eyes as the canoe slipped over the edge. It felt like a rollercoaster ride, but when she came up out of her seat, nothing was there to hold her inside. As her stomach filled with butterflies, Heather sprang out of the canoe and tumbled into the pounding water at the bottom of the falls. Then she strained upward. Just as her head broke the surface, however, it hit something hard. Reaching up, she felt the seat of the overturned canoe!

Heather pushed against it to free herself, but the damaged craft had lodged on a rock. She also discovered that she had to stand on her tip-toes to keep her head above water.

I can't stay like this forever, she thought grimly. *I hope someone finds me!*

Suddenly she heard a knocking sound, and the canoe shifted slightly, pressing her backward into the water. Heather screamed.

* * *

"Hey, where's Heather?" Jenn asked Pete as they carried their canoe along the path that skirted the rapids.

"Wasn't she right behind us?"

"She was when we were on the water. I don't see her anywhere now," Jenn's voice trembled.

"Let's stop for a minute," Pete suggested, and they put down the canoe. "Hey, Evan!" he shouted. But his friend couldn't hear him over the laughter and conversations. Pete finally walked over to his buddy.

"What's up?" Evan asked.

"We don't know where Heather got to."

"We'd better look."

But Heather was not among their group, and the chaperons were getting worried.

"Where could she have gone?" Mrs. Lynch asked Sarah.

The athletic director frowned beneath her dark sunglasses. "Maybe she broke away to explore that side stream."

"Heather wouldn't do that!" Jenn defended.

"If she did, though, what should we do to find her?" Mrs. Lynch persisted.

"Let's leave our canoes here so they don't slow us down. This path goes past the falls. If Heather got on the rapids by mistake, that's where she'll be," she explained.

As they rushed toward the falls, Jenn told Pete, "I wonder what makes Sarah so sure Heather went this way."

"I'm thinking the same thing," he replied suspiciously.

"How far is it to the waterfall?" Evan asked Sarah.

"A couple hundred yards," she called out.

When they arrived on the scene, Jenn let out an ear-piercing shriek. Just under the cascade, the mountain boy hovered over Heather's capsized canoe.

"He's drowning her!" Jenn wailed. "Someone stop him!"

Evan cannon-balled into the foaming water, opting not to dive head-first because of the rocks. Pete and Mr. Lynch followed his example. By that time, Evan had pushed the mountain boy aside. As the youth fled into the woods, the three men tried to free the canoe from its rocky perch in the cold water. When they gave the final push, Evan pulled Heather to shore and sat her against a tree where she caught her breath. Pete and Mr. Lynch dragged the disabled craft to the bank.

Heather's honey-brown hair clung tightly to her head. Besides being drenched, her hiking jacket and pants were torn in several places. There were cuts on her face and hands. Jenn took off her jacket and put it around her friend's shoulders.

"Heather, why did you go the wrong way down the stream?" Mrs. Lynch asked. "Sarah warned us about that."

"My canoe got really hard to steer, and I just kept drifting toward it," she said. "Someone tried to rescue me, and I thought it was one of you. But then I heard you all calling and shouting."

"It was that mountain kid," Pete said.

"I thought he was trying to drown you," Jenn commented.

"So did I," Evan agreed.

Heather couldn't have been more surprised. "What happened to him?" She was dying to question the boy.

"He took off for the woods," Jenn pointed.

"Who is he anyway?" Mr. Lynch asked Sarah.

"Oh, just some pesky kid who hangs around," Sarah replied. "We'd better get Heather back to the campground before she catches cold out here."

I bet she knows more than that, Heather thought. She had no idea why the boy tried to rescue her, though, or how he had known she was in trouble in the first place.

An hour later Heather stood at a sink in the rest room toweling her hair vigorously. Mrs. Lynch had sent the weary teenager and her three friends back to the dorms to rest. Evan and Pete helped Sarah bring back the disabled canoe. The others had gone on with their trip.

"What I wouldn't give for my blow dryer," Heather sighed. "And my poor clothes. This is the second set I've ruined this weekend." But that didn't destroy her spirit of adventure. "I know how we can spend the rest of the day," she said a few minutes later.

"You're supposed to be unwinding, remember?" Jenn teased.

"Remember what?" Heather joked. "Anyway, I want to check out that canoe I was riding in."

"Do you think someone tampered with it?" Jenn's blue eyes widened.

"Possibly. I mean, why did Sarah insist I use that particular boat, then get me to stay by myself in the rear?"

"I wouldn't put it past her and her pals," Jenn pursed her lips.

"I'd also like to find that mountain boy. Because he attempted to rescue me, I'm confused about him. Maybe he's not in on Sarah and Drew's plot after all, but then, who is he? And where will we find him?"

"Well, I'm game," Jenn announced.

"Good for you! Let's get the guys when I finish up in here."

It was still well before noon when the foursome set out to find answers to Heather's pressing questions. Their first stop was the boat shed where they found Woodie working on the damaged canoe. His expression was serious as they approached him.

"What is it, Woodie?" Heather urged.

"The last time I saw something like this," he shook his head, "was in the war."

"What happened?" Evan moved closer.

"This boat should never have been taken out."

"What do you mean?" Heather questioned.

"It had a weak spot on the bottom," Woodie explained.

"I noticed the canoe was leaking way before I hit the rock," Heather mentioned.

"There's something else," the older man pointed out. "If you look closer, you'll see the letters C-H-M-A and the number six on the bow."

The teenagers examined the overturned boat as it rested on two wooden sawhorses. Heather became excited when she saw the letters. *I bet they're an abbreviated form of "chominiska,"* she thought. "The 'six' is painted on, but someone made the letters out of tape," Heather said aloud.

"Uh-huh," Woodie nodded. "I don't know what this is all about, but we don't have canoes with that registration."

Heather became grim. "I believe someone disabled this canoe and made sure I would be the one using it." *Probably Sarah, Drew, or Hawk,* she thought.

"Why would anyone do that?" Woodie asked innocently.

"You tell us," Evan challenged.

13

Little Cabin in the Woods

Heather stared at the handyman in anticipation, wondering how he would respond to the challenge.

Woodie shrugged. "All I can say is that you're not the only ones who've been hurt in this fiasco. I am sorry, though, that this had to spoil your trip, Heather."

"It's not just this canoe thing, sir," Evan said respectfully. "What about yesterday when that bear and the mountain boy nearly chased Heather off a cliff?"

"I know, I know," Woodie said.

"I believe that some people are deliberately sabotaging this camp," Heather told the man. She didn't go into further details just yet.

Woodie seemed surprised. "I never thought of it that way," he remarked. "I just figured it was bad luck."

"That's what Camp Mohican's enemies want you to think. They want the Fennimores to go down without a fight," Heather explained. She began twisting a piece of her hair. "I think you can help us."

"I'd be more than glad to," Woodie stated. "If what

you're saying is true, well, it's just not right."

"For starters, there are these mysterious letters taped to the canoe," Heather pointed out. "They remind me of the word *chominiska.*"

"Oh yeah," Jenn nodded enthusiastically. "I see that, too."

"What in the world does *chomin*-whatever-it-is mean?" Woodie asked.

The teenage detective told him how *chominska* had appeared on a tree near the sight of the bear attack that summer. Then Heather mentioned the flashlight and snake incident with Dick Walker on the first night and how someone had scrawled the word on a tree near his tent.

"It had to have been someone who knew where we'd be camping that night," she concluded.

"Like Sarah Cooper," Jenn said in disgust. "She also went ballistic when I found a piece of paper in her room with that word on it."

"I don't know what it means, that's for sure," Woodie said sadly, "but from what you're sayin', Sarah must have changed."

"I think she got mixed up with the wrong man," Heather commented.

"Drew Hayward?" Woodie raised his gray eyebrows.

"Exactly. At least that's what Sarah's brother says."

"You know, I'm no gossip, but this could be important," the older man said reluctantly.

"What?" Heather coaxed, hoping for a good clue.

"Duncan Cooper was here today."

"He was?" The teenager was surprised. "What was he doing?"

"Arguing with his sister, I'm afraid." Woodie paused, then continued. "Every time he comes here, Duncan just seems to bring trouble with him. First the Fennimores threatened him with a lawsuit over the interstate, then Duncan and Sarah started arguing about it, too."

"Is that what they fought about today?" Evan asked.

Woodie shook his head. "I couldn't say. I didn't want to know."

Heather was deeply interested in this. "Woodie, do you think Duncan could have been trying to steal Camp Mohican from the Fennimores for his gain?"

The handyman pursed his lips. "I really don't think so. I got the impression he was just doin' his work, you know. And that he was concerned about Sarah and that Drew fellow." He looked very sad.

"So you don't know what *chominiska* means?" Pete returned to that issue.

"Can't say I do," Woodie shook his head.

"If you're innocent, then why are you going to work for Sarah and Drew at their new ski resort?" Jenn asked bluntly.

Heather would have preferred a more tactful approach, but she admitted to herself that she had been wondering the same thing.

Woodie lifted his right hand. "I give you my word of honor that I've done nothing against the Fennimores," he said solemnly. "I only agreed to work for Sarah and Drew 'cause I like her and this place a whole lot."

I think Woodie's okay after all, Heather thought. Her friends were heading toward the same conclusion.

"What about that mountain boy we've been seeing?" Evan went in that direction. "Do you know anything about him?"

"I know who you mean, but I've only caught glimpses of him now and again," Woodie told him. "He seemed a bit odd. Real quiet fellow. I think he scared some people, especially Kelly."

Heather told him how the boy had acted when her canoe lurched over the falls. "At first Evan and Pete thought he was trying to drown me. Now I think he was only trying to help." She frowned. "If he really were here to make trouble, he could have made plenty at that point. I wish I knew what he's all about."

After discussing this for a few more minutes, Heather said she'd like to find out where the boy lived and why he was always hanging around. The teenagers asked Woodie if they could borrow two canoes.

"I don't see why not," he said.

Woodie accompanied them to the lakeside dock where he chose two sturdy canoes for the group. Then he returned to his chores, and the young people set off to find the mountain boy. Their first stop was the waterfall.

"I'd like to examine the area where he ran after you came on the scene," Heather explained when they arrived. "We might find clues that will lead us to him. This mountain boy is real sneaky, though. When Kelly saw him the other night at our tent, he left no traces."

"Isn't that another reason you didn't think he shot my tire?" Evan asked.

"Exactly," she answered. "That person ran away so recklessly that he smashed those tree branches and left obvious footprints. This kid, on the other hand, knows the woods."

"He may be good," Pete said as he crouched low to the ground, "but this time he left in too much of a hurry. Look."

The husky blond pointed to damp imprints on a dirt path leading into the woods. They seemed just the right size for the mountain boy.

Heather became excited. "This is great, Pete! Let's follow them!"

After a mile or so, there were no more tracks to follow. The teenagers appeared to be no closer to finding the intriguing boy.

"Terrific!" Jenn lamented. "Just when we were getting somewhere, too."

"Now what?" Pete asked.

Heather suddenly lifted a finger to her lips and said, "Shh! I hear something."

Her friends tensed, listening quietly.

"I think it's two men talking," Evan whispered.

"The voices are coming from that direction," Heather gestured.

When she parted some hemlock branches to get a better view, the teenager's eyes widened in amazement. "Will you look at that!" she exclaimed quietly.

14

Confrontation

Y ou're in my way, Heather!" Jenn protested in a loud whisper.

She and the guys pressed closer to Heather to see what had so fascinated their friend.

"It's the mountain boy." The teenage detective moved aside for them to see. "He's with a strange-looking man, who's a giant."

"Get a load of that cabin!" Pete sniffed. "It looks like Abraham Lincoln lived in it."

"Maybe it's that Hawk guy," Evan suggested.

Heather shook her head. "I've seen Hawk's picture. That's not him."

"The boy and whoever his friend is must live here," Evan commented. "There's a wood pile by the door and smoke coming from the chimney."

Heather smiled. "Nice work, Evan."

"You've even got him thinking like a detective," Jenn laughed aloud.

A little too loud. Immediately the mountain boy and

his companion stiffened. Their ears were acutely sensitive to the woods—they knew an intruder lurked nearby. The boy automatically reached for his bow and arrow. The man grabbed a pistol from his jacket.

"Maybe we should leave," Jenn fretted.

"I think she's right," Pete agreed. "I mean, they have weapons, and we don't. Besides, he's enormous! What do you say, Evan?"

"It sure would be nice to know what they're up to," he murmured. "Besides, if we make a run for it, they might get the wrong impression about us and attack."

"Oh," Jenn sang the word nervously. "Let's get out of here."

"They're heading this way," Heather announced calmly. "Let's go talk to them."

"Are you out of your mind?" Jenn hissed. "They'll kill us!"

"I doubt it. The mountain boy had his chances at both the Pinnacle and the waterfall and didn't take them. I really think he's harmless."

"That bow and arrow don't look harmless to me," Jenn stated.

Heather separated the hemlock boughs and stepped into the clearing. Evan followed her.

"Hello!" Heather called out, approaching the men.

The mountain boy breathed a sigh of relief. The man, who was around thirty-five and looked fierce with his thick, black beard, put the gun back. In spite of the cool afternoon, he only wore a thin jacket over jeans and a white tee shirt that said "Greenpeace" in faded letters.

The mountain boy, also wearing jeans and a tee shirt, stood a little behind him and to the side, like a shy child. Up close he wasn't frightening at all. He was only around thirteen. The boy gazed at the trees where Jenn and Pete had remained.

"There are two more," he told the man, pointing.

"Come on out!" Heather yelled. She nearly laughed as she watched Pete coax a reluctant Jenn to leave her spot.

"They're okay," the boy said.

The man nodded. "Forgive us for the rude welcome," he said.

"That's all right," Evan spoke up. "Sorry we startled you."

No one said anything for a few moments, and everyone felt uncomfortable. Then Heather made introductions. "I'm Heather Reed, and these are my friends, Evan Templeton, Jenn McLaughlin, and Pete Gubrio."

The man nodded. "I'm Buck Jameson, and this is my nephew, Nate."

"We're here with a group from our church near Philadelphia," Heather continued, surprised by the man's introductions. "Some strange things have been going on at Camp Mohican, and we're trying to find out why."

"The Fennimores are selling their camp to a man who's going to build a ski resort here," Pete blurted.

"Yes, I know," the man remarked coolly.

"You know?" Heather's eyes widened in disbelief.

He nodded. After a momentary hesitation, he invited them to the cabin to talk. The teenagers chose to sit on the wooden porch, rather than go inside.

Buck inhaled deeply. "I'll start at the beginning," he said, leaning into a homemade rocking chair. Nate picked up a piece of wood and began whittling. "I moved here two years ago after I left teaching. I was a biology professor at Penn State."

Heather and her friends were listening closely.

"I'm experimenting with plants from this region. The Delaware Indians used many of them as medicine, and for a long time I've wondered how well they worked," Buck explained. "The other professors thought I was a crackpot. When my department wouldn't pay for my research, I quit and came here."

"That's interesting," Heather commented. "You obviously didn't build this cabin, right?"

He shook his head. "It's very old."

"It's also on the Fennimores' property," Pete pointed out.

"Yes, I know," Buck muttered. "I plan to pay them for using the place when I can get a grant for my experiments."

"And Nate?" Heather nodded toward the mysterious boy.

"He came to live with me this spring," Buck explained, lowering his voice slightly. "His parents both passed on, and I became Nate's guardian." He offered no explanation for what had happened, and the teenagers didn't pry. "He loves it here."

"What about school?" Evan asked. "Where does he go?"

"He doesn't," Buck replied. "I home-school him. Nate's a quiet, shy, boy. He doesn't like to talk more than he has to and keeps pretty much to himself—except for one thing." The boy's face went red as his uncle explained, "There's a girl at the camp he thinks is cute. It's Katie, right, Nate?"

"Kelly," the boy murmured.

"Ah, yes, Kelly." Buck addressed the visitors again. "Nate overheard a camp counselor plotting against this girl's family. It had something to do with forcing them to sell the place. Nate became concerned and stayed within shouting distance of her all summer in case she needed to be rescued." The man grinned. "He's very glad she came back this weekend."

"That explains a lot." Heather was deeply satisfied with the information. "Tell me, Nate, was that counselor's name Sarah Cooper?"

The boy looked down at his feet and kept whittling as he nodded wordlessly.

"Was she alone?"

"No," he spoke.

"Were there two men helping her?" Heather described both Drew Hayward and John Hawk.

"Yes," he responded.

"Was there anyone else that you know of?"

Nate shook his head decisively.

"What about Woodie, the handyman?" Evan questioned. "Is he okay?"

"Yes."

Buck described the various plots Nate had heard the culprits discuss during the summer. "He also learned about the gang's use of a code word. It was to alert each other where to strike next."

"*Chominiska?*" Heather asked excitedly.

Nate nodded.

"What does it mean?" Jenn pressed.

"I don't know," the boy said.

"The two men used to meet behind our cabin, and Nate learned other things as well," Buck continued.

"Like what, Nate?" Heather asked.

"Well, they spread many rumors about the camp," the boy said as if talking were painful for him. "They always blamed it on the girl's brother because he worked for the state."

"Sarah's brother?" she pursued.

"Yes."

"But he had nothing to do with the rumors?"

"No," Nate said. "He only wanted to keep Sarah out of trouble. The Fennimores didn't like him, though."

"Because of the interstate?" Evan questioned.

"Yes."

"Those guys probably made the harassing phone calls and sent nasty letters to the Fennimores, too," Heather reflected.

"Uh-huh," Nate confirmed. "They also weakened the chains holding up the swing that the little boy got hurt on. Then they messed up the kitchen for that health inspector and canceled food orders."

"What else do you know?" she asked eagerly, surprised by all he had overheard.

"The guy named Hawk has followed you this weekend," he said. "He and the others heard you were coming. They had read about you in the papers and were afraid you'd ruin their plans."

"How do you like that?" Jenn retorted.

Now Nate spoke more freely than before. "He and Drew have tried to run you off the camp. Hawk scared your leader with that snake and even damaged your boat so you'd be afraid and leave," he told Heather.

"What about Friday night when I saw you and that bear near the Pinnacle?" she asked. "I thought you were going to kill me with that bow and arrow."

"That was no bear." He stopped whittling.

"What do you mean?"

"That was John Hawk dressed like one," Nate spat. "He's also the one who the campers spotted this summer. I meant to drive him away, not hurt you."

"Wow!" Evan and Pete said in harmony.

"Imagine that!" Jenn exclaimed.

"Do you know anything about the bow-and-arrow attack on my Bronco?" Evan asked Nate.

He shook his head. After Evan explained what had happened, the boy guessed that Hawk and Drew had done it to make him look guilty. "They heard Kelly and many others were afraid of me this summer," he said. "They probably wanted you to think of me as a criminal so you wouldn't focus on them."

"I've got it!" Heather suddenly cried out, startling everyone half out of their wits.

"I hate it when you do that," Jenn said, putting her hand over her heart.

"Sorry, but I just realized that *chominiska* is an anagram. It's 'Mohican' all jumbled up."

Evan frowned. "But what about the three extra letters, *i, s,* and *k?*"

"Ski!" Heather yelled triumphantly.

"Ski Mohican!" Jenn laughed. "What a genius!"

"So the mystery's solved, right?" asked Pete.

"Wrong," Heather said candidly. "We still have to catch Sarah, Drew, or Hawk in the act of sabotage so the police can arrest them. That is not going to be easy."

15

Last Chances

Heather's next move was to ask Buck Jameson if she and her friends could borrow Nate. "I think he can help us capture Sarah and her gang. Besides, I'd like the Fennimores to hear what he has to say. Maybe then they'll believe they're not the victims of bad luck."

"That's fine with me," Buck announced. "It'll be good for him to be around some young people for a change."

Nate had his own life vest, and after he got it from his room, he and the teenagers left in their canoes. Their first stop was the campsite where the trail group had just sat down to lunch. As Heather introduced Nate to everyone, she saw Kelly Fennimore's look of disbelief. *I can only imagine what she must be thinking right now,* she smiled to herself.

Over sandwiches Nate apologized shyly to Kelly. "I'm real sorry I scared you this summer," he told her. "I only meant to protect you from those people."

Kelly smiled back. "And I'm sorry I misunderstood

you so badly. I'm glad you'll be helping catch Sarah and her thugs."

Then she sighed. "I just wish I could go with you. Dick and my dad are doing fine out here without me, but my parents don't want me hanging around with you, Heather."

"Do they think I'm such a bad influence?" her friend grinned.

"Just the opposite! They think I'll poison you with my conspiracy theories," she said in a disappointed tone.

It was difficult to talk much more about the mystery with Kelly because her parents were too close for comfort. Following lunch, Arlene Fennimore insisted that Heather return to the camp with her close friends.

"You shouldn't be out running around like this after your accident," she scolded. "Take her back and make sure she relaxes," the woman told Jenn, Evan, and Pete.

You're probably just trying to keep me out of trouble, Heather speculated.

Although Mrs. Fennimore seemed uncomfortable around Nate, she didn't object to his returning to Camp Mohican with the teenagers. Heather wanted to tell the Fennimores about what Nate knew, but this wasn't the time or place. Dick Walker figured they were just trying to be nice to the boy. He was always encouraging youth group members to invite new kids to their events. The five young people paddled back to the main camp discussing how to trap the young villains.

"We could just call the police and let Nate tell them what's going on," Pete suggested.

"That probably would work at home where we know the police," Heather replied. "Here they might think it's just another Mohican-related prank. Besides, they probably wouldn't take a bunch of teenagers seriously."

Pete nodded that he understood.

When they arrived at the camp, Heather made a proposal. "Let's walk around the grounds just to see if anything unusual is going on."

"I think that's a good idea," Evan agreed.

"Aren't we supposed to make Heather rest?" Jenn teased.

The others laughed. "I can rest later," Heather said impatiently.

Since the stables were the nearest building to the lakefront, they wandered over there. Just as they were about to enter an open side door, the young people heard Sarah inside yelling. Heather waved them to a window where they discreetly peeked in to see what was going on. Mohican's athletic director was on a portable phone.

"I don't want your help!" she stormed. "Don't call me again!"

Sarah hung up and angrily threw a metal pail against the side wall closest to Heather and her friends. They ducked, but droppings from a shower of oats rained upon their heads.

"I hate you, too!" Sarah screamed at a beautiful black horse.

Heather was the first one to look back at the disturbing scene. She saw, to her horror, that Sarah was about to kick the animal. The teenager shot right up and rushed into the stable.

"Stop!" she yelled at the top of her lungs.

Sarah froze in mid kick. Then she turned her wrath on Heather. "What are you doing here, you little busybody?" she hissed.

"You have no right to abuse that horse," Heather charged.

"Get out of here before I abuse you!" the young woman threatened, taking a step toward her.

Suddenly Evan appeared, followed by Pete, Jenn, and Nate. "I wouldn't try anything if I were you," Evan warned.

"What in the . . . ?" Sarah's voice trailed off.

Then her mood swung abruptly in the other direction. She slumped onto a bale of hay and started crying. Heather and the others watched in startled surprise. They didn't know what to say at first. A few minutes later Heather broke the silence.

"I think you'd better tell us what's up."

"Why should I?" Sarah sniffed.

"Because we know what you've been trying to do," Heather stated.

Sarah lifted her head and swiped at her tears with the backs of her hands. "You and my brother," she shook her head. "You never let up, do you?"

"Was that him on the phone?" Heather asked.

"He wants to help me," Sarah nodded. Then she laughed spitefully as she stared at Heather. "I was afraid you'd find out. We tried to get you out of the way, but you wouldn't take the hint."

"We?" Jenn asked.

"Might that be you and Drew Hayward and John Hawk?" Pete specified.

"Why should I tell you?" she asked, once again peevish.

"Maybe the police will go easier on you if you do," Heather stated.

"Police?" Sarah looked totally dumbfounded. Then she became visibly frightened—and willing to cooperate.

"Yes, police," Jenn said sarcastically.

Heather thought about the missing pieces in the mystery and questioned Sarah about them, hoping she would talk. "Nate has already told us most of what happened, but there are still some unanswered questions."

"Like what about my tire?" Evan demanded. "Do you know about that?"

Sarah admitted that she did. "I set that up. I told Hawk where to find you after Arlene Fennimore asked you to make that pharmacy run."

"So you made it look like I did it?" Nate spoke up. He was angry.

"Yes." After a pause she pleaded with them not to call the police. "I don't want them involved," she stuttered.

"You should have thought of that before you got into this mess," Pete said in disgust.

"I, I know," Sarah whispered. She looked up from where she sat. "My brother kept telling me the same thing."

"Speaking of Duncan," Heather prodded. "You'd better tell me how he's been involved, too."

"In spite of what some people thought, he didn't have anything against the Fennimores," Sarah told her. "Drew thought he'd want to get back at them for their lawsuit over the interstate. He asked Duncan to help us, but my brother refused."

"So that's how Duncan fits into this," Heather said.

"Now what?" Evan asked.

"We need to catch Drew and John in the act of sabotaging the camp," Heather said.

"I could just testify against them," Sarah said grimly. "Wouldn't that be enough?"

"Not really. You're an accomplice, and the guys could always say it was your idea. It would be your word against theirs."

"The case would be stronger if the police actually caught them red-handed," Evan concluded.

"Well, that shouldn't be difficult," Sarah remarked.

"What do you mean?" Heather's pulse quickened.

"They had a 'plan B' just in case the canoe accident didn't scare you away."

"Or drown me," Heather glared.

"I'm sorry," Sarah whispered. "That wasn't my idea. I just followed Drew's instructions."

"And just what is 'plan B?'" Jenn demanded.

Sarah looked up from her hay pile. "If Nate knows what's going on, he probably told you about that fake bear." They acknowledged that he had.

"I'm curious about something. Wasn't he injured when Nate shot an arrow into his arm?" Heather asked, remembering that awful night at the Pinnacle.

"He wasn't hurt that badly," Sarah informed them. "I patched him up." She took a deep breath. "Mrs. Fennimore—the older one—is going to ask you and your friend," she inclined her head toward Evan, "to take the tents and food to the backpackers late this afternoon. Woodie has to pick up the canoes, and Mrs. Fennimore thought of you because of the Bronco."

"And?" Heather nudged.

"The bear—actually Hawk—plans to attack you on the way to the trail," she continued. "Drew will back him up, and they'll make the incident look like a mauling."

"How?"

"By beating you, then scratching you up a bit." She was quick to add, "Drew wouldn't try to kill you."

"How comforting," Heather shuddered.

"I guess we should go along with the plan," Evan suggested. "We can notify the police and have them waiting in the wings."

"I think that's our best bet," Heather agreed. "They'll probably believe us, now that we've got Sarah to testify."

"Let's do it," Evan said. "What have we got to lose?"

"Camp Mohican," Heather muttered darkly.

"Your lives," Jenn echoed.

16

"Bear" Necessities

How dare you!" Mrs. Fennimore shouted after Sarah told her story. Kelly's grandmother started toward the athletic director, but Mr. Fennimore took his wife firmly by the shoulders.

"I said I was sorry," Sarah whined.

"Do you know what you have put us through, young lady?" Mr. Fennimore's lips were white with fury.

"I know." She stared at her boots.

"I'm calling the police," Mrs. Fennimore said, pulling away from her husband's grip. "I want all three of them arrested right now."

"Please don't just yet," Heather begged.

"Why not?" Mrs. Fennimore's fiery eyes demanded an explanation.

"If you let us go along with Drew and John's final scheme, the police can catch them in the act," Heather pointed out. "Then there'll be enough evidence to convict them."

"I think I see what you mean," said Mr. Fennimore.

"And what if you get hurt?" his wife countered.

"We shouldn't, not with the police following closely."

"How will they know where to find you?" Mrs. Fennimore persisted.

Sarah interrupted. "I was supposed to let Drew and Hawk know where to strike by writing a code word on a tree along the road."

"Chominiska?" Heather raised her eyebrows.

"Yes," Sarah said.

"Whatever are you talking about?" Mrs. Fennimore demanded.

"It's an anagram of 'Ski Mohican,'" Heather explained. "That's what you were going to call your resort, wasn't it, Sarah?"

"Uh-huh. We also used the code in case any of us got cold feet." She paused. "I often did."

"I don't get it," Jenn said.

"It was supposed to remind me of my reward so I didn't back out of their plans," she explained. "Anyway, Drew and John will know where to strike."

"You could call the police and explain the situation," Heather told the Fennimores. "They need to be brought on board, and I doubt they'll believe a bunch of kids."

"And what about her?" Kelly's grandmother pointed at Sarah.

"Would you please ask them not to arrest her until the men are caught? She can tell the police where to find the attack site. Besides, if Drew or Hawk try to get in touch with her before then, and she's gone, they might take off," Heather said.

Mr. and Mrs. Fennimore reluctantly agreed to this plan. They summoned the local police, and Sarah made a full confession. In the end, the officers decided to have Mrs. Fennimore keep tabs on her after the athletic director showed them where Drew and Hawk planned to strike. The police didn't want to call attention to their plot by taking Sarah away or leaving a policeman behind with her.

Sarah painted *chominiska* at the lower end of a tree truck near the access road. The police agreed to send two plainclothesmen there around four o'clock.

At three-thirty Mr. Lynch knocked on the door and asked for Heather. "I wonder if you and Evan would mind taking supplies to the campers?" he asked stiffly, as if he were playing a part in a drama and wasn't too sure of himself. "Woodie's busy getting the canoes that got left behind on today's outing."

"Sure," Heather agreed, her heart thumping.

Within minutes, she and Evan left their other friends. Jenn and Pete gave them thumbs-up. Nate simply stared as they walked away.

"Well, here goes nothing," Evan told Heather after packing the Bronco.

"Are you nervous?" she asked as he pulled onto the road.

"A little," he admitted. "Are you?"

"Yes, but I'm mostly excited. It's wonderful to think that the Fennimores will get to keep Camp Mohican after all."

"I wonder if they'll make any changes," Evan mused.

"I wonder, too. You know, I think Drew and Hawk had the right idea about making the camp into a ski resort. Camp Mohican is in an ideal spot for skiing, and the new interstate will bring them a lot a business."

"It's a nice old place, though," Evan rebutted. "As terrific as a ski area would be, I'd hate to see the old camp totally dismantled."

"I guess we'll just have to wait and see. Besides, we need to catch these thugs first."

"Do you have any doubts?" Evan glanced at her sideways.

She exhaled. "You never know."

He reached across the gear shift and squeezed her arm. "We're in good hands," he said, looking upward.

As they neared "ground zero," Heather's palms grew sweaty. She took off her mittens, but her hands remained clammy. Just then they heard a growl.

"That sounds like the real thing," Evan commented tensely.

"Maybe he took lessons," Heather joked. "We'd better look afraid."

"That shouldn't be too hard," Evan mumbled.

Both of them hoped the police were nearby when the phony bear finally charged out of the woods. Heather screamed.

"A bear!" Evan exclaimed, as it came toward them and stood in front of the Bronco.

"Let's get out of here!" Heather yelled.

"Maybe I should run it over," Evan threatened.

Suddenly "the bear" opened the driver's door and pulled Evan out, kicking him in the ribs. Heather could hear Hawk swearing under the costume. She rushed out of the vehicle and tried to pull Hawk off Evan. The muscular man reached back and tossed her aside as if she were a doll. At that moment, Drew Hayward appeared from behind the tree marked *chominiska*.

"There's no way you're going to mess up my plans," he spat. Drew's intense green eyes were full of hatred.

"Let's teach them what's what around here," Hawk grunted. Standing over Evan, he peeled off the bear outfit and tossed it in the bushes.

"That was stupid," Drew derided. "Someone might find that."

"I'll get it later," Hawk promised. "I have business here."

He seized Evan by the left arm and pulled him upwards, causing the teenager to wince in pain. Drew collared Heather and shoved her in the direction of a footpath.

"Where are you taking us?" she demanded indignantly.

"Figure it out if you're so smart!" Drew sneered.

As their tormentors pushed Heather and Evan down the narrow pass, she wondered where in the world the police were. *Didn't they find the place?* she thought. *If they don't get here soon, it may be too late for me and Evan!*

Bramble bushes tore at their hiking pants, and branches swung into their faces as their captors flung a steady barrage of threats at the two teenagers. In the meantime, Heather sensed that she had been this way before. A few minutes later, she knew.

"Recognize it, do you?" mocked Drew as he took her to the very edge of the Pinnacle. "It isn't a neat way to go, but it's very efficient."

"Let her go!" Evan demanded.

Drew countered with a punch that knocked him out cold.

"It'll make our work easier," he said matter-of-factly.

"Monster!" Heather jeered, still standing upright.

"You're not going to get to me, you little pain-in-the-neck!" Drew charged.

"Aren't we going to claw-mark her first? You know, make it look like a real bear attack?" Hawk asked hopefully. He produced a large hunting knife, and Heather shuddered.

"She's pretty scratched already, and we can't stay here much longer," Drew cautioned.

"I can do a quick cut—right across her face." Hawk hovered closer, and Heather backed away.

"Don't go too far, or you'll go over the edge." Drew laughed scornfully.

As Hawk moved toward her, Heather instinctively raised her hands to protect her face. Suddenly someone grabbed her from the side and knocked her down. Heather hit the dirt with a loud thud, a cloud of dust temporarily blinding her. As she coughed and choked, she could hear men fighting. Her vision started clearing then, and Heather saw two men tangling with Drew and Hawk. She assumed they were police officers. Then she saw Evan on the ground and still unconscious, his head and arms hanging way too far over the edge of the Pinnacle.

I've got to help him! Heather thought desperately.

She grabbed her friend's boots and pulled him back with all her might. When Hawk took a swipe at her, though, Heather couldn't hang on any longer. She feared Evan would fall to his death!

Swiftly one of the new men knocked Drew out with a blow to the head. He scrambled after Evan. Before he could get to him, however, Nate Jameson burst onto the scene and pulled the teenager to safety. That freed the men to deal with the thugs. Moments later, they snapped handcuffs on Drew and Hawk and started reading the scoundrels their rights.

"Thank God you got here when you did," Heather gasped. "What took you so long?"

"We got held up chasing a speeder," the shorter one explained. "Sorry. We didn't understand how serious this call was."

"Are you okay?" she asked Evan as he started regaining consciousness.

"Yes," he croaked. "You?"

"I'm fine now," she smiled, taking his hand.

"Who's the kid?" asked the lead officer.

Heather introduced Nate Jameson. "He's a life-saver," she praised the "mountain boy."

After the culprits had been arrested and Sarah taken to police headquarters, the elder Mrs. Fennimore cleaned and bandaged Heather's and Evan's wounds. Her husband summoned a doctor, who carefully examined both teenagers and announced that they had sustained only minor injuries. When word of what had happened reached Dick Walker, the youth group director immediately brought his backpackers to the main camp to spend their last night there. Everyone was eager to hear everything about the mystery from start to finish as they sat around a spectacular bonfire.

After they sang songs and were about to make s'mores, Kelly's mother got up and made an announcement.

"My husband and I are so proud of you young people for saving Camp Mohican," she began. "Let's hear it for Heather Reed and Evan Templeton!"

The other campers clapped wildly as the two teenagers blushed.

When the group got quiet again, Arlene Fennimore said, "I also want to ask my daughter's forgiveness. I didn't take her seriously when she told me about a conspiracy. It almost cost us this camp. I'm sorry, Honey."

As Mrs. Fennimore hugged her daughter, followed by Mr. Fennimore and his parents, the campers said, "Aw" in unison.

"I'd also like to thank Nate and Buck Jameson," Mrs. Fennimore concluded. "Mr. Jameson," she turned to Buck, who had joined them earlier, "my in-laws have decided to let you stay in the cabin rent-free until you get on your feet financially."

"Thank you," Buck said humbly.

Then Kelly's dad said, "There's one more announcement. We've decided to give lifetime camp memberships to Heather, Evan, Pete, Jenn, and Nate."

"Then you're going to keep the camp?" Mrs. Lynch asked when the applause died down.

"Yes. We'll operate it as a camp in the summer and a ski resort in the winter."

When everyone had eaten at least three s'mores and the singing resumed, Evan told Heather, "You were great today."

"You, too," she smiled.

"You've done it again," Jenn clapped Heather on the back.

But Heather's mind had already begun to wander. She couldn't wait for her next adventure.

ABOUT THE AUTHOR

Rebecca Price Janney has dual careers as both a writer and a teacher. In addition to her *Heather Reed Mystery Series,* she has had numerous articles published in newspapers and magazines, including *Seventeen, Guideposts, Decision, Moody Monthly, World Vision, Childlife, War Cry,* and *The Young Salvationist.* Her published work also includes a section in *Shaped by God's Love,* an anthology published by World Wide Publishers. As a teacher at Cabrini College, her speciality is Jewish and Middle East History. Rebecca and her husband Scott live in suburban Philadelphia.